MW01504093

Producer & International Distributor
eBookPro Publishing
www.ebook-pro.com

Shadow Soldier
Roni Eliav

Translation from the Hebrew by Itamar Toussia Cohen

Contact: ronieliavbooks@gmail.com
ISBN 9798685842206

SHADOW SOLDIER

RONI ELIAV

IN LIEU OF A PROLOGUE

This is a story about Erez Eliav— a boy, a soldier, and a man. Erez Eliav does not exist outside the pages of this book; I wish he had, since we share many values and convictions. He's my kind of guy, I'd love to invite him for a pint of beer at the beach.

The events described in this book are also fictional. But similar events might have happened to someone, yours truly included... The book contains no new insights or revelations regarding covert operations and events, nor about military strategy and tactics, and holds no unknown secrets.

This is not a book about one particular unit or another. Rather, this is a book about a soldier who served in an elite unit— a soldier who has aspirations, succeeded, and failed, but never gave up. He mostly followed his convictions, and, like anyone, made many compromises along the way.

Although the story is fictional, this book is personal. I could definitely have been Erez under certain circumstances. I know many people who have a little bit of Erez inside them. Not heroes— but warriors. And yes, sometimes they enjoy the warrior's life. Either way, it was Erez's character who directed my writing. I hope you will enjoy reading them as I enjoyed writing them.

I would like to thank more people than brevity permits.

This book is dedicated to my real brothers-in-arms and to my beloved wife, without whom none of this would have been possible, as well as to my squad-commander— the legendary Nachum Lev— who tragically died in a motorcycle accident.

CHAPTER 1

PURSUIT

August, 2000. A military base south of Nablus, the West Bank. Erez, 42 years old, is an army major on reserves duty. Company commander.

The night guard shook Erez awake. He groggily glanced at his watch. It was 4:45, still early. It would be at least another half hour before the rest of the soldiers woke up, had their coffee, and started loading up the trucks. Erez always hated waking up, both in the service and at home. But on reserve duty he made sure to be punctual. His position as company commander was dear to his heart; he could never quite explain to Lauren why that was. She hated the army, and viewed his reserve duty with contempt. Her European upbringing was different than his, and she couldn't wrap her mind around the Israeli devotion to and camaraderie of the reserve army.

Erez rose to his feet and started dressing meticulously: he put on a new pair of socks, comfy pants, and clean underwear, and applied a generous amount of anti-chafing cream. Just as he was finishing up, Jacob – his long-standing signaler – came in holding two cups of coffee. Erez thanked him, lit his first cigarette of the day, and the two of them walked out into the hustle and bustle of the company preparing for its assignment. Groggy soldiers walked past them, lethargically loading combat-vests, weapons, and helmets on to trucks, and then heading over to Albert, the veteran company's cook, to get a strong cup of coffee. Albert could have delegated coffee-making duties to a staff soldier, but it had always been his habit to wake up with the rest of the company and follow them wherever they went, preparing their meals and maintaining a personal rapport with each and every one of them.

"It's a good company," Erez said.

"Looks like you're going soft," Jacob remarked.

"Have been, for a while now," he glanced over at his aging companion.

"Yes, but only on the inside," Jacob said.

"Well, you gotta maintain your image," Erez concluded. "Come on. Let's go."

***

Ibrahim Nasser lay in a cave in the side of a cistern, his AK-47 and a bag of cartridges and magazines kept tidily by his side. He was thinking about Yusuf-Ali, whom he had sent along with his cousin to carry out a suicide bombing in Jerusalem.

"In a bus full of children," he instructed, "to hurt and humiliate the Zionists."

Ibrahim felt no pangs of conscience. His uncle had gotten him into this organization, and Ibrahim had taken his place after the Jews killed him in his home. Ibrahim lived outdoors, in the open terrain. He had no intention of repeating the same mistakes his uncle had made. He would enter the surrounding villages only under cover of night, to brief his foot soldiers, stock up on supplies, and dispatch operatives to carry out attacks. The rest of his time was spent out in the rugged expanse. As far as he was concerned, Jews were city-dwellers who didn't know the first thing about the surrounding land. An Arab had every advantage out in the field. Jews were spoiled, over-reliant on technology. Ibrahim had become the stuff of legends among villagers, and his name travelled as far as Headquarters in Nablus. They wanted him to move to Nablus, but he was apprehensive. In the open terrain he was untouchable, but there, in the city, he'd be easy prey. The Israelis were after him, turning over every stone, interrogating his family. He lay awake, excitement coursing through his veins in anticipation of the attack that was about to be carried out. But he was nervous as well. The Jews are weak and spoiled, but they are vengeful and organized, and they have all their gadgets and contraptions, he thought to himself. If he wasn't careful, they might arrest or kill him. But not today. Today he'd hide out here, and tonight his cousin would report back to him.

***

The disorderly manner in which the soldiers unloaded the trucks irked Erez. It's a lucky thing the enemy is inferior to us both in quantity and quality, otherwise we'd be done for by now, he thought to himself.

Erez gestured for the platoon commanders to come over to him.

"Yom-Tov, you stay to my right. Nadav and his platoon will be on my left. Eran, you trail in the rear, ready to move in. Maintain your lines, and divide your platoons into smaller squads. I remind you – this is a live-fire scan. If you come across something unusual or suspicious – fire at will. Just maintain your lines so we don't shoot at each other. Hand-grenades are to be thrown only under your express orders. Remember to report as you progress. Any questions?

"What about breaks?" one of the commanders asked.

"In coordination with me. Get a feel for your men. If they start to tire, let me know and we'll stop. Remember, these guys aren't so young anymore."

"Neither are you," Eran teased. He was young, but the team now under his command was once Erez's, and Erez gave him preferential treatment.

"Let's have a race when we get back, I'll show you old."

"Sorry, I don't pick on geezers."

"Alright, alright, enough with the nonsense. Let's keep this tidy, and hopefully we can catch the son of a bitch today," Erez concluded.

The soldiers put on their helmets and combat vests. Using silent hand-gestures, the officers organized the platoons into a broad line and prepared to start scanning. Each band had a soldier trailing slightly behind, to provide safety in case of an ambush from the rear or to join in as backup in case of head-on combat.

Erez gathered his command post in the center of the hill that was about to be scanned by the company, and cocked his M16 rifle. The sound echoed across the line, as the soldiers cocked their own rifles in reply. He pointed forward, and the long line started moving together.

"Jacob, report we've started."

Jacob gestured to Erez that he got it, and relayed

the message to headquarters. The thunderous sound of rounds going off echoed through the silence as soldiers shot into the bushes before checking them. Erez delighted in the scent of gunpowder filling the air. The thrill of the hunt made him feel strong and formidable.

That feeling stood in complete contrast to the gloomy mood he'd been in lately, since coming to the realization that he had to shut down his startup company. With each passing day, it became increasingly clear there would be no new investors, while existing investors were losing their patience. Erez fought ferociously to save his company, but expenses were mounting and income was dwindling. Eventually, he'd had to throw in the towel and admit he'd failed. He gathered his employees and announced that the company was shutting down. He then faced the few investors left, and made sure the process was completed in an orderly manner. The warrant summoning him to reserve duty could not have come at a better time. This is what I'm meant to be doing, he concluded, bittersweet. I'm a predator, not a clerk.

***

In a different place at the same time, Gal and Shunit got on the bus to school as they did every day. They were fraternal twins, ten years old. Gal was starting to hit puberty, while Shunit was still firmly preadolescent. Their developmental disparity was reflected in their relationship, with Gal becoming increasingly dominant, while his sister grew slightly clingy.

"You see that guy, two seats in front of us?" Shunit asked.

"What about him?" Gal wondered.

"He looks suspicious," Shunit asserted.

"You're just imagining things. Mom says we feel insecure because Dad's in reserve duty."

"Mom thinks everything that's wrong is because Dad's on reserve duty," Shunit shrewdly remarked.

They both giggled. The issue of reserve duty had become a constant bone of contention between their parents. The kids tried to stay out of it. Gal was proud of his father, the army major with the imposing rifle; Shunit missed his warm embrace, so she tended to side with her mother.

"Gal, that man scares me. Let's get off."

"What are you afraid of?"

"A terrorist. You remember what Dad told us. Why would he wear such a heavy coat in this heat?"

"You're just imagining things."

"Gal, please."

"Fine. We'll get off at the next stop."

***

After an hour of scanning, the eagerness and fighting spirit was starting to die down. The sound of rounds going off was becoming less frequent, and the soldiers were sweating heavily. It was only 7 AM, but it was clearly going to be a scorching hot day.

Erez called for a water break. The soldiers dropped right where they stood and started passing water canteens among themselves. Erez slumped down alongside Jacob and Yair, and looked ahead. They were on the side of a mountain, and to their left ran a channel with a nice, clear path. Above the channel, an Arab village crowned the mountaintop. Israel Border Police was keeping the village under curfew that morning. A path snaked down from the top of the mountain, patrolled by jeeps of the regular Combat Engineer force stationed in the area. The mountainside rolled on for three miles, eventually coming to a fork and splitting off into two channels. An armed lookout kept watch over the fork. Intelligence insisted that Ibrahim Nasser was hiding out on this mountainside.

"You're a fickly son of a bitch," Erez muttered to himself, "but we'll get you this time."

"You want candy?" Yair asked while peeling the plastic off a lozenge-shaped army sweet.

"No thanks. You shouldn't have any either. It's bad for your teeth, and it's fattening," Erez replied.

"Sorry to disappoint you, Erez, but my teeth are already rotten and I'm already fat."

Erez looked over at his friend, who was already starting to lose his hair and had indeed grown chunkier. Yair was a successful accountant, and it seemed that sitting all day behind a paper-laden desk suited him well. Still, he always made it to reserve duty. Company soldiers who needed his professional assistance were always welcome, and paid when they could. Surprisingly, most of them never exploited his generosity. Erez sullenly recalled he owed Yair money for work he'd done for the company. Yair never mentioned the debt, but Erez felt he had to make an effort to repay him quickly.

"Alright, let's move. Let's try to get this bastard before it gets really hot," Erez got up and gestured to Jacob with a slight tilt of his head. After so many years together, Jacob knew what Erez wanted. He let all the platoon commanders know they were moving and informed the command post.

***

Ibrahim awoke abruptly to the sound of boots shuffling and rounds going off. He grabbed his AK-47, but immediately realized how futile that was: one Soviet-era assault rifle against dozens of state-of-the-art American M16s. They couldn't be looking for me, nobody knows I'm here, he tried to reassure himself.

He listened in silence – the commotion was definitely heading in his direction. Voices were growing louder and clearer. They can't find me here, they wouldn't dare go into a cistern. Yes, the Jews were cowards – the thought comforted him, but he remained alert.

Suddenly an explosive roar ripped through the air. Ibrahim immediately realized that was the sound of his hopes shattering. They really didn't go into cisterns – they chucked grenades down them. The image of his body blown to bits flashed before his eyes. How did I ever think to trap myself in a hole with no exit! he thought to himself as he clasped his head tightly.

Out of the depths of despair, he came to a decision: he would go out and face them. He would surely get killed, but at least he'd die like a hero.

Ibrahim Nasser clutched his weapon, slung his bag over his shoulder, and stopped for a moment to listen again before heading out. They were really close, but, for some reason, they had stopped moving.

***

The bus pulled into the station and Shunit rushed towards the exit. Gal reluctantly followed. "We're gonna be late to school because of your hysterics," he grumbled.

Shunit turned around to reply, but from the corner of her eye she spotted the suspicious man reaching into his heavy coat. She desperately tried to force her way to the exit. Gal reached out to grab her.

The explosion ripped through the dense air on the bus, sucking up the oxygen and building into a giant fireball. Whoever survived the initial blast died of asphyxiation. 54 people were killed, most of them children, and ten more were wounded.

***

"Erez, command post wants you to drop everything and get over there."

"Tell 'em I'm busy," Erez replied.

"I did, but they're adamant."

"Get rid of them," Erez insisted.

"They say it's about your kids…"

Erez froze in his tracks, panic flooding his body. The world seemed to move in slow motion: he noticed the strained faces around him, the light breeze cooling the sweat on his face, and the grey and white stones resting against the backdrop of the deep crimson earth. A thorny burnet bush pricked his calf through his fatigues.

***

Erez mourned his children in his foreclosed house. His debtors had reluctantly agreed to delay the foreclosure for a week. Every day, streams of people came to console him. No one really had anything to say. Each of them, depending on who they were and their relation to Erez, tried to reach out to him, but he was utterly indifferent. In spite of her own grief, Lauren tried to break the ice – but Erez just sat there like a zombie, stiff and unresponsive. He nodded once in a while, and occasionally smiled to himself for no apparent reason. Guests gossiped about him out in the balcony. "He's in shock," they whispered to each other as they left the house, "he can't process what happened." Every evening, men from the nearby synagogue came to the house to join in the evening prayers. Erez participated unshaved, unbathed, and with his shirt-collar torn, as Jewish tradition dictated. He prayed thoughtlessly, mechanically going through the motions, lost in the depths of his anguish and despair.

The funeral was a horrifying experience. Two tiny coffins, nearly empty as there wasn't much left to bury. There had been no bawling and wailing on his part, only silent weeping. Erez said the kaddish prayer with a hollow voice and a blank stare. Ilan, his younger brother, took care of everything, and comforted their mother who was sobbing uncontrollably. Erez walked ahead of the procession; outwardly seeming composed and collected, but inwardly collapsing into a dimensionless black hole.

On the third day of mourning, in the evening after everyone had left, Lauren turned to Erez and said: "I'm going back to Germany, to my parents." He stared back at her with a sealed expression, without uttering a word. "I can't take this place anymore," she said in broken Hebrew, "this country has sucked my happiness dry." She switched to English, as she always did when she spoke emotionally: "There's nothing left between us. You don't need me and you don't enjoy my company, while I loathe your love for the army and war, and this disgusting country." She erupted into tears.

Erez wanted to hug her, but couldn't. He felt as dry as a piece of plywood about to be cast into the fire. Deep inside, he wanted to tell her that they still had each other, and that love would prevail. But all he could muster was: "You're right."

The next day, she hugged him and kissed his cheeks. He inhaled the scent of her shampooed hair one last time, and she was gone.

That was the way she'd always been, independent and impulsive. Erez had loved her for those traits. They'd lived like two bachelors even after they got married. Having the kids forced her to somewhat settle her roaming spirit, prompting her to adopt some semblance of a schedule. Underneath all the sorrow, she's probably breathing a sigh of relief, Erez bitterly thought to himself.

I should also feel free, he mused. But Erez didn't want to be free. All he had ever wanted was a family, a house and kids, to feel rooted in place. Now I don't even have a house anymore, he dejectedly thought to himself.

On his way to the bathroom he looked at himself in the mirror. He saw his reflection, red-eyed and unshaven. He became angry when he realized he felt sorry for himself, and looked away. A moment later, he turned back to face the mirror. His pupils constricted. He stared into the seeds of anger that had appeared in his eyes.

That day, soldiers from the company came to the house, walking in slowly and awkwardly, unsure whether to shake his hand or offer a hug.

"Did you get the bastard?" Erez asked.

"No, we called off the scan when you left."

"That's too bad. Intelligence was absolutely certain he was there."

That afternoon he was visited by fellow officers,

including the regiment commander and division commander. Erez felt warmly enveloped and safe. These were men he respected, who trusted and believed in him. In the absurd order of promotion in the reserve army, one of them had been under his command at one point, while another went to officer's school with him. He felt at ease when speaking with them, taking comfort in the familiarity of comrades-in-arms. To his own surprise, he found himself opening up about his debts, about Lauren leaving, and how in a week's time he'd be out in the streets.

"Why don't you come back into the service?" Eitan suddenly proposed.

"Who'd take an old geezer like me?"

"We're the same age," the division commander protested.

"They'll never take me," Erez said, a small trace of hope lingering in his voice.

"You jackass, who're you talking about? I'll take you!" Eitan said. "I could use an officer to coordinate special operations."

Erez stared at him, shocked to realize the offer was real.

"Well, mull it over…" Eitan retreated, clearly misreading Erez's expression.

"There's nothing to think about! You have your special

operations officer," he said, smiling for the first time in a week. "Wait, what rank do I need to be for that position?" he asked, immediately realizing how ridiculous it was to worry about that now.

"Well, you'll have to be bumped up to lieutenant colonel. But I think you're due for a promotion anyway," Eitan replied.

CHAPTER 2

ORIENTATION

It seems I had gotten used to the idea long before I was drafted to the army.

I think the moment I realized I would like being a soldier was when I read the novel Battle Cry by Leon Uris. I was about 15 years old. I enjoyed the book so much that as soon as I finished reading it, I immediately went back and read it again. I read it over and over, practically memorizing it. I absolutely loved that book: a diverse group of young people coming together to fight for a cause they believed in. Being a young kid pumped with hormones and a Zionist education, I bought into that wholeheartedly. The concepts of fraternity and camaraderie-in-arms struck a deep chord with me.

Israel experienced two significant wars when I was growing up. The first was the heroic Six Day War. The fear and anxiety that had gripped the country before the war broke out were replaced with an adoration of the army and soldiers. I was nine years old and easily impressible. A couple of years later, during the Yom Kippur War, my experience was totally different. I was 15 years old, and enlisted along with other kids my age to help in hospitals and other essential services. We did everything from collecting garbage in the mornings, helping farmers in their fields, and digging trenches which turned out to be completely unnecessary. But what all of us really wanted was to be out there on the front lines, where the soldiers were throwing themselves into the fray to protect us. During that war, we encountered grief and bereavement for the first time. It scared us, but at the same time made the whole thing all the more heroic.

I grew up in Ashkelon, a poor peripheral city on the southern coastline near Gaza, a city which, despite its troubles, is blessed with a long beachline, sprawling sand dunes, and bountiful, raw, untamed nature. My parents were Holocaust survivors, a fact they vehemently denied. My grandfather fought in the German army during World War I, where he lost both his legs. After the war, he somehow made his way to the Jewish community in Romania, where the cripple was married off to a mute. Subsequently, my father grew up with the harshest contempt towards any display of weakness, a trait he passed down to us. My mother's story remains shrouded in mystery; we know that she originally came from a Jewish-German family, but we don't know much more than that, other than the fact that her whole family was wiped out in a concentration camp. She somehow managed to survive and was later adopted by a Jewish-Hungarian family. She instilled in us a need for survival.

I was the middle child between a bright and talented older sister, and a brilliant younger brother, smart as a whip. They both excelled in their studies. I, in turn, played basketball and soccer, I ran, I climbed, and I fought. At best, teachers said I had "potential." Dyslexia was not a term anyone used back then, but in hindsight it played a decisive role in my childhood.

In the summer before the Yom Kippur War, I went on a one-month squad-commander's course in the Gadna – a military-preparation program for Israeli youth operated by the Israel Defense Force. The course was held in Sde-Boker, a kibbutz deep in the southern Negev Desert. Lines of tents were pitched along the edge of a cliff commanding a majestic view of the Zin River. They treated us like soldiers, but with a slightly softer touch. It was there that I realized I was a pampered boy: it was my first time not having my mother around to do my laundry for me, iron my clothes, and cook my meals; my first time without the comfort and safety of my house, my room, my bed… Nothing. It was just me and my knapsack. I found out that I didn't do so well in structures, and that I really didn't like being told what to do. At the same time, I discovered the intoxicating smell of the desert at night, and the joy of being part of a group. I was a bit shocked to learn there were stronger and fitter boys than me. Eventually, I also experienced the unbridled joy of returning home and resuming my daily routine.

I started training. I didn't know too much, but I was motivated. I ran in the soft, loose sand on the beach, over the dunes, through thicket and brush, across fields, in water, uphill, downhill. I ran in the mornings, in the afternoon heat, in the evenings, and at night. I ran until I couldn't go any further, and then carried on anyway. I did pushups and sit-ups every day, all day. I did 500 pushups a day, a figure that sometimes rose up to 600 and even 800.

I got stronger. My endurance grew, and my confidence followed. I became leaner and taller. 6 feet tall, packing 168 pounds of pure muscle. I played every sport I could: I practiced judo with judokas, played basketball with basketball players, ran track and field with athletes, did karate, and played soccer. I looked for people to challenge me in the streets, at school, and in the youth movement – resulting in brawls more than once. More often than not, though, things were settled amicably. I adopted a hardline approach to life – nothing was too difficult, no challenge beyond my reach. I failed often, sure, but I picked myself up, dusted myself off, and tried again – persisting until I succeeded, or at least until I reached a satisfactory point.

I read a lot, mostly adventure stories, but not exclusively. I read adventure novels set in the American Wild West by Karl May, historical novels by Mary Renault about Alexander and Theseus, Graves' "The Golden Fleece"; Howard Fast novels like "My Glorious Brothers" and "Spartacus"; Defoe's "Robinson Crusoe" and Edgar Rice Burroughs's "Tarzan". In those years, science fiction books were just starting to come out in Hebrew: I gobbled up Asimov and Arthur C. Clarke, Bradbury and Bester, and of course Roger Zelazny and his mythical characters, and Larry Niven's masculine heroes.

I developed a classical-romantic worldview without actually having received a classical education. I yearned to live a warrior's life, but pretty early on I understood there was a difference between being a fighter and merely being someone who fights. I gradually came to realize that without a value system to guide you, you're not a warrior – you're simply a rabid dog on the loose.

I came to understand that combat was a choice rooted in one's character, one that had to be undergirded by a coherent set of values and a moral code. This was a long process, with at least as many downs as there were ups. But as my conscription drew closer, my values and priorities began to crystalize: I believed in integrity, honesty, justice, and in defending the weak; but also in defending and pursuing what was mine – such as self-respect, competitiveness, and self-discipline, alongside independent and critical thinking. More than anything, I believed in taking accountability for my decisions and actions and those of the group to whom I belonged. Perhaps at the time these thoughts weren't finely articulated, but even in their raw form – they were very clear to me.

There were many events and occasions where I honed my worldview: field trips, sporting competitions, true and not-so-true friendships, little betrayals, and teenage rebellions; summer jobs, sports classes, youthful romances, getting piss-drunk for the first time, and partaking in all manners of unruly behavior; navigating through structures and institutions that didn't get me in the slightest, winning and losing.

At some point during high school I came across the name of a mysterious unit in the army. The name was unclear, but what was certainly clear was that this unit represented the cream of the crop – the most elite unit of them all, and it was top-secret. I read about special operations carried out in North Africa during World War II, and the pre-independence Palmach unit of the Jewish underground army. My imagination ran wild. There was almost no information available about it, which made it all the more appealing for me. I tried to find out how I could join it, but all I could find were bits of contradicting information and a lot of fake rumors. Eventually, I learned that I would need someone to recommend me. I had trouble finding recommenders – wherever they were, they weren't in Ashkelon. After conducting extensive research, I managed to locate three such recommenders. Later, I found two more. That miniscule number was due to the fact that the unit was mainly associated with people from the labor settlement movement, namely from the Kibbutzim and the agricultural settlements. Some hailed from cities, mainly Jerusalem, but not very many from Ashkelon.

I managed to find a potential recommender nearby, a brother of a friend who also wanted to join the unit, but he refused to recommend me. My dad told me he knew someone whose son could be a recommender. To my great surprise, that information turned out to be true. So we went over to his house, and he agreed to recommend me. I immediately found another one, a friend of my sister. I had two recommendations, now all I had to do was pass the examinations.

I found out everything there was to know about the

examinations. I was told we would fill sandbags and carry them up a hill – so I filled sandbags and carried them up a hill. I was told we would run on loose sand – so I planned a crazy track that included running through the ruins of an old Arab village, scaling the imposing sand dunes, and running through their soft sand for two miles – all in all three miles one way, and then three miles back. I ran that track three times a week.

Finally, I received my summons to the examinations. I got up early in the morning and took the two-hour bus to the Wingate Institute – more specifically, to the military base adjacent to the national sport institute, overlooking the sandstone bluffs above the Mediterranean Sea. I didn't know it back then, but that military base was the army's main fitness center, where I was destined to spend weeks upon weeks in grueling and highly gratifying training.

About 300 people from all corners of the country arrived with me. I saw the occasional familiar face, whether from the youth movement or the Gadna, but I was mostly just by myself – except for one person who had come with me from Ashkelon, but quit pretty early on. We were divided into groups. The gist of it was simple: we were assigned tasks and exercises, and the examiners watched and took notes. The first task was to lug sandbags, of course. I happily filled a sandbag and was the first to reach the hilltop with it slung over my back. As I ran down, I passed the other examinees huffing and puffing as they labored their way up. I realized I could carry two bags at once – a combined 110 pounds. I filled two, tossed them over my shoulder, and started running up. Within an hour, I had amassed an impressive heap at the top of the hill. During one of my rounds, I noticed someone trying to steal one of the bags from my pile. I immediately pounced on him, and he bolted. Another time, as I was running up, I could hear the other guy from Ashkelon asking one of the examiners: "What does it take to pass?" The examiner pointed at my pile and said: "That, to start with."

Later, we were egged on by the examiners to quit, and some did just that. The next exercise was a run in the loose sand. I had a blast. Training in the soft-sand dunes in Ashkelon had built up my calves and quads. The track was challenging, but not as much as the one I was used to running at home. I came in first by a wide margin. The examiner asked me where I was from, and I could see the look of surprise on his face when I answered Ashkelon. The city was renowned for crime, violence, and backwardness – not exactly a place you'd associate with excellence.

The tasks and exercises carried on until dusk – I had excelled at them all. To my surprise, my energy levels never dropped: I was tired, but ready for more. At that time, I didn't yet appreciate the electrifying power of motivation. At the day's end, they called eight names – mine included. They told us to go home and come back the next day, to a green shack next to Army Headquarters in Tel-Aviv.

I wasn't sure how to react. Going all the way back to Ashkelon only to make the long journey back early the next morning seemed like too much of a hassle. I considered just spending the night on a street bench in Tel-Aviv, until a group of four friends from a kibbutz in the south offered me to stay with them in an apartment their kibbutz owned in Tel-Aviv. It was my first encounter with the kind of military camaraderie that would become my way of life over the course of the following years.

The next morning, we located the green shack. They asked us many questions, and we had to fill out a bunch of questionnaires and personality tests. Then each of us was interviewed by a psychologist.

"Close the door," he told me as I sat down.

"I closed it when I came in," I replied without turning around. I was tipped off they would play that trick, so I took it in stride.

"What will you do if you don't get accepted to the unit?" he asked.

"I believe I will be accepted," I replied with a feigned air of self-assurance.

"And if you won't?" he insisted.

"Then I'll try again."

"And then?"

"Again and again."

"It says here that you're a candidate for pilot's training. That's very prestigious."

"If you have the forms here, I'll waive my candidacy right now."

"You're going to have to do that at the Air Force's office. But don't you want to be a pilot? With the winged pin and the hat? That's every Israeli's dream."

"I want to be a fighter."

"And a pilot doesn't qualify as a fighter?"

"Maybe. But not the kind I want to be."

"And what kind is that?"

"I want to be a field soldier, a shadow warrior. I want to do things with my own hands, not through machines…"

He looked at me and said: "You'll have the opportunity to do that, I believe, but not necessarily here."

The interview concluded. I went home a bit confused: on the one hand, I felt I'd fared well, but on the other I didn't really know what they were looking for. Two weeks later, the phone rang, and it just so happened that I answered. The girl on the other side of the line asked to speak with me. When I confirmed it was indeed me speaking, she quite dryly informed me that I was invited to the unit's Gibush – its advanced selection process – and that I would receive a draft warrant by mail. I hung up the phone and stared at it incredulously, half-expecting it to ring again and for someone to tell me it was all a prank.

I was absolutely elated. I wanted to shout from the rooftops, but I was warned that I wasn't allowed to say anything to anyone. So I only told my parents and my girlfriend. They didn't see what all the fuss was about.

After that, I had my high school matriculation exams. One day, on the bus ride over to school, we heard that a special unit of the army had rescued the Israeli hostages who'd been held in Uganda, and that they were flying back home. Suddenly, everyone was talking about this special unit. I didn't dare say that I was halfway there.

The exams were over, we had our last hurrah, and one by one my friends went away to the army. Somehow, I found myself volunteering at Mesilot, a kibbutz in the Beit She'an valley, working the fields during the day and partying with my girlfriend and buddies during the night. We were being totally exploited, of course, working for nothing but food and board. But we had a blast, and enjoyed being out of our parent's houses.

I later travelled to an isolated beach in Nuweiba on

the eastern Sinai Peninsula. It was perfect: the clearest blue water you'll ever see, pristine white sand, one beachfront restaurant, and a bunch of kids camped out in sleeping-bags. I didn't want to go back. The summer was over and the holiday season came, my girlfriend went back to school and I went back to training. My mother stuffed me with home-cooked food and did everything she could to pamper me, while my dad gave me random pieces of advice. I wanted to enlist already.

I tried to get my driver's license, but to my amazement I failed my driving test. I tried again, and failed again. I was embarrassed by the third try, but still managed to fail again. I decided I had a problem with machines, and felt pleased with my decision to waive pilot's training. Then the day finally came. We had our names taken and got on the bus. "You'll be sorry!" soldiers yelled as the bus drove away. When we reached the base, the driver opened the door and said: "Just think about it as a three-year break. It was six, in my case…"

CHAPTER 3

GIBUSH: ADVANCED SELECTION

Back then, the selection process was divided into two parts: one examination day prior to enlistment, and advanced selection immediately after. Those deemed good enough made it to the *Gibush* – the two-week advanced selection process.

We were already soldiers, officially at least. We were signed up, given identification cards, vaccinated, and provided with uniforms, shoes, and a duffle bag to keep our stuff in. We didn't know anything about anything, and had no idea what to do. In the first 24 hours we spent as soldiers, we raked the lawns, picked up litter, and tightened the ropes of our tents. But mainly we sat around doing nothing. Slowly, we started to get familiar with each other. Some were loud, others were quiet and reserved; some read books, while others made up petty contests to pass the time.

Night began to fall, and still no one told us what to do. So we did nothing. Another day went by without anyone paying attention to us. Late that afternoon, a sergeant walked by and incredulously asked: "You guys are still here?" We replied in the affirmative. He left, and never came back. As time went by, the air got tense. We all realized that all of us were competing against each other for the same few spots in the unit.

In the evening, as we got ready for bed, we were blinded by the headlights of two trucks approaching. Two raggedy-looking soldiers came out and told us to gather our stuff and get on the trucks. One of us asked them if they were sure they had the right group, but they ignored him. We got on the trucks and crammed in tightly. After about an hour's ride, we were ordered to alight. We were in the middle of nowhere, in a barren valley surrounded by a dense pine tree forest.

They told us to pitch our tents. It was a simple enough task, but the instructors knocked them down every time we finished: they were either not tight enough, not parallel enough, not the right angle, etc. It started raining, and our mood – which was foul already – declined further. After that, we packed knapsacks, unpacked them, and packed them again. We then ran to and fro, packed again, and then unpacked again. Miraculously, without any prior preparation, I got the hang of packing the bags right from the outset. Eventually, they sent us to sleep. Pup tents are not made for large people, certainly not two of them, but we were exhausted and simply crashed asleep.

We were jolted awake at 5:30 AM. They sent us running, and taught us how to stand during morning roll call. After that, we had a meager breakfast of bread and jam. Throughout the day we ran, moved stones from one place to the other, ran again, learned to fall into different formations, and then ran some more. We were assigned personal weapons from the armory, and were quickly instructed how to field-strip, reassemble and clean our rifles. From there, we went to the range. Since I had prepared in advance by training with the Target Shooting team, I was able to produce a tight shot-grouping that prompted the instructor to ask me my name. That evening we went on a ruck march. The rain picked up again. We didn't know it yet, but it was about to be one of the rainiest seasons in recorded history. Our new shoes were tight and chafed our feet. It was only the second night, but our feet were already covered in blisters.

In the morning, after a solitary few hours of sleep, we woke up only to stand out in the cold for an hour wearing nothing but a thin pair of fatigues. In a friendly tone, the instructors offered anyone wanting to quit to go to the tent and get some hot coffee. Some took him up on the offer, but most of us kept standing in the cold. It started raining, but the instructors didn't budge. They seemed to love it in the rain. We were shivering cold, but kept on standing.

The instructors were fit, muscular and lean. They wouldn't let us call them our commanders, because we hadn't earned the right to have commanders yet. The entire day was spent running, constructing arbitrary formations out of stones and logs, taking them apart, and building them again. At any given moment, we were either running, rolling, heaving, or hauling. There was a small platform next to us with three or four instructors on it, observing us and taking notes.

We were cold, and the food was scant and poor. We had seven minutes to eat. I'm a slow eater, so I hardly managed to get more than a couple of bites each meal. Within two days, our entire company got the runs. We were all constantly running to the latrine at the top of the hill. Every afternoon, a truck was filled with those of us who couldn't take it any longer and quit, shipped off to be "good soldiers, but somewhere else."

One time, they took us out on a ruck march and after about three hours we were scattered in the field and told to run back to camp. Some made it by themselves, others needed directions. I was among those who made it, but just barely. My feet were sore and covered with blisters, and both my Achilles tendons were inflamed from running in heavy army boots. Every night, after an hour and a half's sleep we were shaken awake by screams and shouts ordering us to go out and stand in the cold. We then went back to sleep, and shaken awake again. We didn't have time to develop a rapport with each other, since we didn't have a second of off-time to spend together. The kibbutzniks found it easier to stand out, they were used to living in groups; they knew how to blend in when they wanted, and how to make themselves seen. The elite among them were used to being group leaders. Those who came from the agricultural settlements were stronger, and used to strenuous manual labor. The city kids just dropped out. They were wholly unprepared for the pressure and the group dynamics, all but the most stubborn of them. I was one of those few, but I was completely exhausted. My body was done. Every single motion required sheer mental conviction. I was absolutely dying for a rest. Soon I started lagging behind, just barely keeping up with the group – but keeping up nonetheless.

Despair crept in. How long will this go on? How can anyone take this? Maybe I'm just not cut out for this… I looked around and saw other people around me faring better than I was. Much better, in fact, and it was more than a few of them. I started seriously contemplating that maybe I'd be better off serving somewhere else. Maybe I wasn't good enough to be among the best. Better to be the head of the fox than the tail of the lion, as they say... It was about then that I reached my breaking point. We were instructed to run to an undisclosed point. We ran on a trail up a mountain, and my breath grew shorter and shorter, and the pain in my feet became nearly intolerable – projecting up through my spine to the base of my skull. I slowed down, soldiers overtaking me left and right. I slowed down to a walk, and then stopped completely. I stood there, looking around, realizing that I had maxed out. I couldn't go on.

At that moment, one of the commanders came up behind me, a kibbutznik from the south, tall, lean, and fit. "So, Erez, we're walking instead of running now?"

I didn't answer. I had drifted away, totally absorbed in my own world. He put his hand on my back and slightly nudged me forward.

"Come on, you got this. Start running," he said and ran off, leaving me there on my own.

I planted one leg in front of my, raised the other, and started running. I ran faster and faster, going past the commander and then past the other soldiers. My muscles were screaming, but I blocked everything out. I flew past everyone and was the first to reach the end point. I started doing the drills we were instructed: pushups, sit-ups, short-distance sprints up a steep incline – just like back home. No one could touch me. The commanders who were there were having a good laugh at my expense.

"Erez kicked into turbo-mode!"

"He must be thinking of that chick waiting for him at the end."

"In Ashkelon you learn to run away fast…"

The commander who gave me the nudge stood there smiling without saying a word. Years later, he would be a soldier in the company I commanded on reserve duty. This one time, we were training in the Golan Heights. Around evening time, I was sitting on the ramp of an APC, smoking a cigarette and watching the soldiers come back from training. He came up to me with two other guys from the company, all of whom were my commanders in the Gibush.

"Tough day, officer?" they joked.

"Do you know that you're the reason I'm here?" I asked him.

"Really? How so?" he seemed puzzled.

I tried to remind him of that moment, my breaking point. He didn't remember. He remembered a different moment, one that I'll recount shortly. Since then, I'm not even sure if he was really there or if I just imagined the whole thing.

The rest of the week was easier, like anything you'd start getting used to. Friday evening came along. Army regulations have it that no activities are held between Friday and Saturday evening – the Jewish sabbath. So we had a decent dinner and then just sat around shooting the breeze, smoking and chatting. As one might expect in such situations, hearsay and rumors took up the bulk of the conversation. One guy heard we were near the end, while another guy heard from a rock-solid source that we had another month to go. The third guy informed us that two weeks from now, paratrooper boot camp would be starting and we'd be part of it, while a fourth guy told us the army was opening an investigation into the abuse of cadets, so they were going to shut down the Gibush... Eventually, we retired and went to sleep.

We woke up to a surprisingly pleasant, sunny day. We set up a makeshift boxing ring, and each squad selected a one contestant to represent it. I happily volunteered. I had done plenty of fighting back home, and even a bit of boxing. I knew I had skills. I later discovered that the kibbutzniks didn't know the first thing about boxing.

I was fitted with a pair of gloves and headgear, and was promptly shoved into the ring. My first opponent was the standout figure of the Gibush, the leader among the kibbutzniks – strong as an ox, with a jaw like a brick.

On the ruck march we'd had on Thursday, he set the pace for the group, with no one overtaking him at any point – not even once. I immediately saw he was completely clueless. His head was slung down, his shoulders were raised too high, and his arms were too low.

It was an utter massacre. I socked him left, right, and center. He couldn't defend for the life of him. But he was strong and determined, and wasn't about to give up easily. I was slowly building up a murderous rage, and just went berserk on him, venting all my frustration in a mad blitz. They eventually had to pull me off him.

The others didn't fare any better, some even refused to enter the ring with me. I was the hero of the day, the undisputed boxing champion of the Gibush. All it won me was endless banter, of course…

The following day my commander, who hadn't been there the previous day, came up to me and asked where I'd learned to box.

"In the neighborhood, sir," I replied.

"Are you from Musrara?" he asked.

"No, from Ashkelon."

"Okay, so don't beat us up…"

Since then, tales of my boxing skills ballooned beyond proportion. Many months later, when we arrived at the unit, we were given an outlandish and comical reception. I was thrown into a boxing ring, given a pair of gloves, and was told: "Now, beat everyone who gets in the ring, or else you'll have to face him!"

They pointed towards an utter beast of a man, standing there dark-skinned and shirtless, flashing a set of pearly-white teeth. He was a legend in his own right. But I was young and brash, and instinctively yelled: "Send him in first!"

I would be reminded of that utterance for years and years. That was what my former commander remembered that day in the Golan Heights. It's worth mentioning that I demolished anyone who set foot in the ring that day. They came in knowing in advance that they would lose. Among them was the same kibbutznik I had knocked out in the Gibush. He later claimed that he'd fared better the second time around, but I'm not sure about that. I pounced on everyone who entered the ring in a fit of fury. I learned to tap into the animal core in me, and become the embodiment of sheer brute force.

A couple of years later, I had a boxing champion serving in the company I commanded. We agreed to spar a few rounds over the weekend, just for sport. When the others woke up around noon on Saturday, he was already in the hospital with a couple of broken ribs. I didn't know how to take it down a notch: as soon as I entered the ring, I just switched into killer mode, destroying anyone in my path.

The rest of the Gibush was easier for me. I stood out, and was given leadership assignments; I had hit my stride. And then, just like that, the Gibush was over.

It was another one of those rare sunny days. We were lying in the sun while in the main tent the commanders were deciding our futures. I went into my tent to rest, and suddenly felt a sharp sting in my back followed by excruciating pain. I screamed, and everyone rushed over. They caught the scorpion that stung me, and I was immediately sent with an escort to the hospital.

I came into the emergency room reeking after two weeks without a shower, covered in mud, with ragged, torn-up fatigues. The nurses treated me like I was a Holocaust survivor. They laid me down and hooked me up to an IV. I was in such bad shape that they were wholly surprised to learn the reason I was there was in fact because of a scorpion's sting.

When the IV was finished, a nurse came over to tell me they would admit me and transfer me to another department. I thanked her, and as soon as she left, I got up, put on my shirt, and walked out of the hospital into the car that was waiting for me outside. "Let's go," I said to the driver, who didn't ask any questions. We got back to the makeshift camp in the pine forest, called Kula after an old Arab village that lay in ruins nearby. As soon as I got in, I saw the medic.

"Oh, you're back? Good. You got in," he said, and casually walked away.

I was left speechless. I had missed the selection roll call, and went over to join the rest of those who'd made it. There were 36 left from over 200 who had started the Gibush. Out of everyone who'd been with me that first day of examinations, only one was left.

So that was that. But it wasn't the end, far from it. It was merely the beginning.

CHAPTER 4

THE SHADOW AND THE GHOST: BOOT CAMP

Every soldier begins their military service with basic training, often called boot camp, in which the objective is to break old habits and instill new ones in their place. The process is especially demanding for infantry soldiers, who undergo physical and mental recalibration, during which they are required to endure arduous physical challenges with little sleep or food. It's a long and painful procedure, and there's no easy way through it. We were designated for an elite unit, and were dispersed to undergo basic training among companies of paratroopers at Camp Sanur.

The year 1977 rolled along. We were about to finish boot camp, which had started in November '76. We hadn't even noticed that the year had passed; we were just starting to emerge from that melting pot that turns carefree civilians into hardened wolves, ready to do anything for the pack. We were near Sanur – a picturesque Palestinian village in the heart of the Samaria region. Sanur was also the name of a British and later Jordanian military camp, converted into the basic training base of the IDF's Paratroopers Brigade. It comprised several long white structures which housed whole companies of recruits, latrines which we meticulously scrubbed every morning, and showers which were used sporadically at best.

Winter was tough that year, and for us recruits it was even tougher. We were cold beyond what any us had imagined possible. The rain pounded down on us, thoroughly soaking our already sweat-doused fatigues; the stench of soaked cotton and body odor was overwhelming. The water droplets running down our bodies then crystalized; it felt like we were going to freeze to death.

We were there because we had volunteered, passed examinations and selections, and were sent to boot camp with the prestigious red-boot paratroopers. We thought we were the crème de la crème, but to our surprise, we were all walked over like doormats. We were good kids, highly motivated and in peak physical form. Among us were kibbutzniks, city kids, kids from agricultural settlements, you name it. We were the pick of the litter, desperate to excel. For those reasons, we couldn't fathom why the road to excellence had to be paved with such constant, relentless humiliation.

We ran, we crawled, we heaved and we hauled, we carried each other over our shoulders, and we ran some more. We field-stripped and reassembled our "best friend" – our rifle. We cleaned it religiously, greasing it at night only to degrease it in the morning. We barely got any sleep. We were made to scrub and clean every inch of space around us – except of course for our own bodies. We weren't allowed to walk, we had to run everywhere, even to the latrines. To get food, we had to climb up a 20-foot rope first. We were allowed seven minutes to eat, two minutes to shit, 15 minutes to clean our rifle. And throughout the whole time, we were dealt heavy-handed, cruel, unjust punishments.

I was placed with the historic "Shaked" unit, who weren't part of the Paratroopers Brigade themselves but, like us, had basic training there. Our drill sergeants firmly believed that being cruel and abusive was the only way to "break the boys" and build soldiers in their stead. They might have been right, but it was hell nonetheless. The previous year, a soldier had committed suicide in the bunker next to our barracks. Every night, we had to run over to that spot "one-on-one" – meaning that each pair of runners would alternate carrying each other over their shoulders. When you're on top, your chest and diaphragm get beaten to a pulp; when you're on the bottom, it's all you can do not to buckle under the weight. So every night we'd be ordered to run over and shout "good night" to the ghost of the bastard who had taken his own life in that spot. We had to stay there until the drill sergeant confirmed he'd heard us.

We learned to shoot our personal weapons; we pointlessly carried weighted stretches on our shoulders. We guarded the base at night. "The area is hostile," they told us. Every day felt like an eternity. We refused to break, because whoever did would be the subject of utter, merciless humiliation. There was one guy who broke, and henceforth was called "the ghost." He was housed in the bunker where that soldier had killed himself the previous year. From then on, instead of wishing the dead soldier good night every night, we'd run over to the bunker and shout "good night, ghost!" Another guy lay weeping for hours on the muddy parade ground; every time he stopped crying, we were ordered to dump a bucket of water over him.

Every night, we'd go on runs that would quickly turn into hellish, sweaty cauldrons of shouting and pushing. As time went on, we accumulated fatigue, knocks, niggles, and injuries; we carried the stragglers on our backs. These runs became a desperate fight for survival: anger, animosity and hatred brewed between us and the drill sergeants, between us and the stragglers, the stragglers and the pushers, and so on. Every time we couldn't keep up the pace, we had to start over.

The drill sergeant was God: judge, jury, and executioner. We didn't dare express our hatred of him, even in private. We were too scared; we just wanted to make it out of there in one piece. We knew this nightmare had an expiration date to it, but time seemed to simply grind to a halt. And then, just as we naïvely thought we were getting the hang on it – we went out into the field.

We walked in the rain for what seemed like an eternity. Our feet filled with fresh blisters, and we were soaked to the bone. When we stood still, we shivered from the cold; when we walked, we shivered from exhaustion. We marched on and on to the monotonous sound of boots stomping the dirt, and eventually we started falling asleep as we walked. Whenever someone started veering off, we grabbed him and pulled him back in line; sometimes they'd stir awake, sometimes they'd sleepwalk right through the whole thing. When we did eventually stop, it was literally the middle of nowhere. We pitched our tents in the pouring rain and the blistering cold, punch-drunk from exhaustion. The drill sergeants lit up a couple of tires in the center of the camp to make some heat; the stench of burning rubber was overwhelming.

The place looked like a surreal inferno. They finally sent us to sleep, and we crashed in our tents – only to be woken up again two hours later.

In the field, there was no one to curb the drill sergeants, and they let their sadistic imaginations run loose. We were tumbled down mountainsides in barrels. We built a huge clock out of heavy stones on the side of a mountain, and every hour at night we had to adjust the clock's "hands." One time during an exercise, I accidently crossed another soldier's line of fire. The drill sergeant deemed that worthy of a death sentence. I spent the entire afternoon digging a grave for myself; later, a group of fellow recruits were instructed to load their rifles with blanks and form a shooting line to "execute" me. I was ordered to fall into the grave I had dug and lay there waiting until the resurrectionist arrived – a recruit sanctioned by "the devil himself" (that being, appropriately, the drill sergeant).

The skin on our hands cracked from the mud, rain, and cold. One time, before going home on leave for the weekend, I was told to do pushups and ordered not to wash my hands. By the time I got home, it felt like my hands were paralyzed. I stood motionless at the entrance to my parents' house, the sweet aromas of a home-cooked meal filling the air. I wondered if I still belonged there: I was reeking, filthy, covered in mud, and unable to move my fingers. My mother took me inside and cleaned me up. She soaked my fingers in warm water and soap, dressed up my wounds, and tucked me into bed with fresh linen. Only then, alone in a dark room, did I allow myself to break. I bitterly wept into my pillow. Later, I walked to the dinner table like a cripple. That night, my girlfriend complained that I was scraping her skin. The weekend flew by, and soon enough I prepared to go back to that hellhole. I put my clean and fresh-pressed uniform on, and grabbed my spick-and-span rifle (my father had spent the whole of Saturday morning cleaning it for me). My hands still hurt, but the pain was tolerable. The wounds had begun to scab. Suddenly I felt that it actually wasn't so bad. I would face my tormentors again, but I no longer feared them. I felt that whatever happened, they couldn't break me.

Everything was harder that week, but for me it felt easier. I found myself right in the thick of the chaos: one night, as I was getting ready for the precious few hours of sleep we were allowed, I heard a racket outside. My tent-mate came crawling inside and told me that the guys were going to get revenge on a recruit who'd gotten us all collectively punished that day. I then did something that in my own mind would define me for years to come. I got out of my tent and stormed into the commotion, placing myself between the recruit and the angry mob. "Go back to your tents," I said sternly, and they did. I walked the shaken recruit back to his tent. The next day the drill sergeants, having heard about the night before, tagged the recruit to me – that is, they ordered me to carry him on my back. "From now on, he's your shadow," they said. "As long as there's sunlight or lighting on – he's on your back." And so it was. I couldn't stand the guy, he was weak and whiny. But I wasn't mad at him. To be honest, I was actually quite proud of the punishment. I carried him around everywhere. He would apologize, and I would laugh.

Finally, we went back to Sanur. This time around, everything was different. Those two weeks in the field had changed us thoroughly, and the transformation was complete: we were now soldiers. By no means good soldiers yet, but soldiers nonetheless. We were better at keeping time, we had learned how to divide tasks between us efficiently, how to follow through when needed, and how to cut corners when possible. We had kits prepared in advance for roll call, night sessions, and morning sessions. We had each other's backs.

"The ghost" was back in the bunker. While we were out in the field, he had stayed in the supply tent. He always looked sated and toasty-warm. One time, the sergeants took us over to see him and made us declare we were jealous of him. And we were indeed jealous of him, especially when we were soaked, freezing, exhausted, and exasperated from the constant abuse. But one time our eyes met, and I could see misery, frustration, humiliation, and envy in his eyes. He was envious of us! From that moment on, I no longer envied him, I felt sorry for him. "The ghost" became a living monument to what we could become.

One evening, we were informed that morning roll call would be held on Mount Kabir the following morning. Mount Kabir towered above Camp Sanur, a steep two-hour ascent – three, with a cot on your back. But since it took two of us just to carry one cot, we spent six long, grueling hours to get all the beds up there. An iron army cot with all our equipment on it weighed about 220 pounds; each pair of us awkwardly gripped, carried, pulled and pushed our cots up a near-vertical slope of a mountain with no paths, wading through slippery mud as the wind whipped around and the rain pounded down. Once we reached the peak – exhausted, soaked, sweaty, and shivering – we had to go back down to get the second bed and start all over again. At 7 AM, 30 beds were neatly lined at the top of Mount Kabir, complemented by the sorry sight of 30 ragged, muddy, sweat-drenched recruits. We were thoroughly worn out, but the thought of our sergeant having to make the steep hour-and-a-half climb up the mountain brought a smile to our faces. Morning roll call on a foggy mountainside was a surreal sight that day, to be sure. But we did it… It was stupid and pointless, but we were equal to the challenge. Our sergeant walked up to us with his sleeves rolled up. It was near freezing out, with specks of ice shimmering on the tall grass. "You cold?" he asked me. "Not at all, sir," I lied. He kept me out there standing in attention for an additional two hours, waiting for me to admit I was lying. I refused, and eventually he broke first. Later, my buddy and I laughed all the way back to camp with our beds on our backs.

By the time boot camp drew to a close, the year had passed. But we were so absorbed in our daily schedules, we didn't even notice. It was another uncharacteristically sunny winter's day. We were entrusted to go out on assignment to patrol the outer perimeter of the base. We were unfledged, as green as they come. We walked briskly, commanded by a fitness instructor who was also a combatant. It felt good to be performing operational duties. After scouring the surrounding mountains all afternoon, we sat down for a rest. Our spirits were high. The commander informed us that someone had broken into the ammunition bunker last night, and that we were on the lookout for suspects. We were cracking jokes and fooling around when suddenly Udi told us to be quiet. We sat there for a while straining our ears. All of a sudden, someone yelled: "Runner!" Somebody was bolting it in the valley below us. "I got him," Shachar said and got into shooting position – but something about the runner's movement seemed familiar to me. "No, don't shoot!" I yelled and leaped forward, crossing his line of fire. I won't have to dig my own grave this time, I thought to myself as I darted after the runner. Udi ran straight across one mountainside and Yuval across the other. The runner was below us in the valley, but it was easier to dash in a straight line than downhill.

My breath was getting shorter, but I was fit and kept accelerating. Just before we reached the valley, the runner turned sharply when he noticed Udi and Yuval were about to cut him off. I saw my opportunity, hastened my steps and leaped forward, crashing into him and sending him tumbling to the ground. I got up and pinned him to the ground with my legs, looked down, and froze in my tracks: it was "the ghost," dressed in civilian clothes, a look of absolute madness in his eyes. I looked at him, and once again did not envy him.

Eventually, boot camp to an end, and we each dispersed back to our own units. The training we would later undergo included unbelievable physical and mental challenges – but nothing would ever compare to those excruciating and traumatic three months in which we metamorphosed from children to beasts.

A couple of years later, I came across my drill sergeant, the one I'd promised myself to beat the shit out of if I ever saw him again. I had gained 50 pounds of muscle since boot camp, and was a formidable sight – an "alpha wolf." He looked at me and I looked at him; he seemed small and unintimidating. We hugged like old friends. Years later still, I found out that my boot camp company commander was among those killed in the Tyre Disaster in Lebanon in 1982.

In the mid-1990s, already a major in the reserves, I was sitting in the command post of the West Bank settlement of Yitzhar, coordinating assignments for my soldiers. My signaler came in and said the regiment commander wanted to see me. "I'll get back to him when I'm done," I brushed him off. The message was repeated twice more, and twice more I ignored it. Finally, someone came in and said the regiment commander was here. I realized I had no other choice, and went out to meet him. As I stepped out of the tent, I saw a short but impressive man, exuding self-confidence and authority, surrounded by staff soldiers who clearly admired him. I looked at him and he looked at me; we immediately recognized each other. It was my "shadow." An awkward silence was broken by a mutual pat on the shoulder. Later, we sat down to have some coffee and a cigarette, surrounded by other officers. He told them he spent most of his boot camp couched on my shoulders. That was only half of the story, of course, but I kept that to myself. That man earned his respect in the hardest way possible, starting from rock bottom and climbing his way to the top of the ladder. He was the embodiment of the expression against all odds.

As for "the ghost," I never saw him again. He disappeared, like an extra in a movie. I can't even recall his name… Sometimes I think he never had one. He was simply the ghost.

CHAPTER 5

AT THE END OF YOUR ROPE: ADVANCED TRAINING

The unit's advanced training program consisted of cycles in which cadets learned a new skill, drilled it repeatedly, and were then examined over it. The examinations were tough, and we had to reach beyond our limits to make it through. The weather often played a decisive role.

The winter of '78 was a wet one. It wasn't just rain, but torrential downpours that even the most senior members of the unit couldn't recall seeing before. We were Qualification Course cadets – no longer fledgling recruits, but still far from accomplished combatants. We had quite a bit of warfare, navigation, and fitness training under our belts. We were disciplined soldiers with a lot to prove; we felt every step we took was a test. We didn't dare say so aloud, but inside, each of knew that if we'd made it this far, we stood a decent chance of making it all the way.

Squad assignments are "rolling" exercises – meaning that once an exercise starts, there are no breaks until its conclusion. We spent several days studying axes of advance for a four-day exercise and prepped our gear. Whatever time we had left was spent exchanging rumors and theories about what we were about to encounter in the exercise. We spent all of Saturday sleeping, resting up to preserve our energy. That evening we held roll call to inspect and weigh our equipment. My gear weighed a hefty 145 pounds. My own body weight was 190 pounds at the time, so my squad commander had no qualms about authorizing me to carry such a load. That Sunday afternoon, following the usual grueling fitness training session, we hopped on a truck and were on our way.

I sat all the way in the back and just chain-smoked the whole ride through, like I always did before any-thing important. It was a relaxed, joking atmosphere at first, but eventually everyone receded into themselves in preparation. Some napped, others read, while others still stared blankly ahead.

We started off with a land navigation exercise. We had studied a 12.5 by 12.5-mile sector, and were now dropped off at a random point somewhere in that sector

without a map. From there, we had to first orient ourselves, then move forward. It goes without saying, of
course, that all this was done in the pitch dark of night.
We were supposed to be dropped off in helicopters, but
we had to change to trucks because of the weather. We
sat at the back behind a closed tarp cover, trying to guess
where they were taking us.

We were dropped off on a dirt road in the middle
of nowhere, somewhere south of the Palestinian city
of Hebron. We were three soldiers, each carrying 70%
of our body weight on our backs. It was a cloudy, dark
night. After a short while, it started drizzling. In that
moment, at the very start, you feel tense and alert, excitement building up in your chest; you feel alone and
cold, but you know that soon enough, once you get into
it, you'll feel nothing at all.

The trick about land navigation is memorizing the
diagonals: paths, roads, streams, power lines, mounds,
and channels. We studied and measured them. We expected the dirt path to follow the northwestern azimuth,
between 330° to 350° on the compass.[1] But instead, it
followed azimuth 250°. We carried on, hoping the difference was only a bend in the road, but the path refused

---

1   The compass divides the 360° of the horizon into four quad-
    rants: 0° directs north, 90° directs east, 180° directs south, and
    270° directs west.

to conform to our expectations. About a mile later, we had to admit that it wasn't the path we thought it was. After talking it over, we decided to head north off the path.

The rain grew stronger. We got out our rain-ponchos. A poncho is a great thing: it's sealed and helps trap your body warmth. The problem is that you sweat profusely in it, so you get wet anyway; it also traps your body odor, so after a while the stench becomes substantial.

After a couple of miles we ran into a ravine which went in the direction we thought it should, so we followed it. Shortly afterwards, the channel split as we anticipated, so we were certain we were on the right path. Now that we were oriented, we picked up the pace. We had to reach the rendezvous point by 2 AM. Gilad and I walked fast, but the third member of our squad started lagging behind. Every time a gap opened up between us, Gilad and I stopped to let him catch up.

The path became increasingly muddy and difficult, and we started feeling the weight on our backs. We each carried our platoon-level weapons: I carried a 50-inch long MAG machine gun, 22 pounds of cast iron. But what really weighed me down was its heavy metal ammunition belts. We were sweating like hogs; the wind and rain beat down on us relentlessly, we could hardly see a thing.

We reached the rendezvous point soaked and sweaty. We were among the first ones there, so we had to wait in the pouring rain for the other guys to arrive. Our assignment was to take over a fortified position. We were well drilled, so the exercise went over smoothly, except for one hiccup: as we retreated in a line formation, Yoram suddenly disappeared into the earth. There was a well there, and the poor guy simply fell in. Luckily enough, he came out bruised but without any broken bones. He sat out the rest of the exercise, and we split back into squads.

At dawn we found a thick shrubbery and concealed ourselves in it for cover. We fell asleep, exhausted. The rain kept pouring down all the way through to midday, when we woke up. We sat there wet and miserable, gnawing on beef jerky, discussing the coming night's assignment.

When night descended, we packed up our backpacks – substantially heavier after soaking up rain for hours on end – and started walking. The first few steps were a nightmare of aching bones and muscles. Our bodies squeaked and squealed, and it felt like we couldn't take another step. But slowly our muscles warmed up, and we picked up a satisfactory pace.

The previous night's problem repeated itself. Gilad and I walked at the same pace, and the other guy couldn't keep up. After a frustrating couple of hours walking, the third guy sprained his ankle. We pounced on the opportunity: we radioed in that we were leaving him behind and that the command post should come pick him up. It was different back then, a time when you could leave a debilitated soldier alone in the field, a stone's throw away from a Palestinian city. Unburdened by him, we were able to walk at a much faster pace. The rain wasn't nearly as bad that night, but it was bitterly cold so we hardly stopped walking.

We completed that night's assignment without a hitch and moved on, eventually reaching the scheduled rendezvous point. To our surprise, our squad commander brought with him the other guy's backpack, and demanded that Gilad and I split his gear among ourselves.

The extra weight made a difficult situation seem almost impossible. I felt my body driven into the ground with each step I took, as if someone had turned gravity up a notch. The strain on my back and knees was unbearable. When we started ascending a slope, my thigh muscles felt like they were about to burst. That night we walked from the Hebron Mountains to Tel Lachish —about 25 miles away.

When morning came, we found cover and dropped like stones. We were panting heavily, as if we'd just finished running a marathon. It took our bodies a while to ease down after the strenuous effort we'd put them through, so we couldn't sleep. When we finally did, the rain resumed with even greater vigor. We cursed under our breaths and tried to wrap ourselves up in our ponchos, but the water easily found its way in and we got soaked to the bone. We couldn't get our body temperature up, and spent the day shivering. Nothing eats away at your energy reserves quite like shivering for hours on end.

When it was dark again and time to move on, we felt absolutely drained. We managed to somehow muster up enough energy to get up, pack up our gear in silence, load up and go on our way. We needed to get to Beit Jamal in the vicinity of Beit Shemesh, about a 13-mile walk. The rain was relentless, and the weight on our backs was overbearing. We tried walking as fast as we could, seldom stopping to drink. During water breaks, we didn't dare take off our gear for genuine fear that we wouldn't be able to get it back on afterwards. When we sat down, we couldn't get up. After every break, one of us had to roll over on his stomach like a giant turtle and push himself up with great effort, and then pull the other up. We were suffering, but still managed to laugh at the absurdity of our situation.

Around Beit Jamal, we started towards the Beit Shemesh engine factory. Even though it was only a couple of miles away, by the time we got there we were drained of our last drop of energy. We found a shrubbery overlooking the factory and once again simply crashed. Our moods picked up during the day. Just one more infiltration exercise and then it would be just a couple of miles to the final rendezvous point. That's not too bad, we thought. We can take it.

It was nighttime. The rain picked up and a strong, cold wind was blowing. On the one hand, conditions were miserable, but on the other hand it made our assignment easier. No guard in his right mind would patrol the perimeter in this weather. I went to deactivate the electric fence, but my fingers were so numb from the cold that I accidently short-circuited the fence. We quickly retreated and took up a hidden position to see if someone would come out and inspect it, but no one did. We assumed they were either put off by the rain, or maybe the rain caused the fence to short-circuit often anyway. We didn't really care. We hurried up, made our way in, planted dummy-explosives, and got out of there.

We loaded our gear and started on the last stretch of this horrendous exercise. I fantasized about the cigarette I'd light as soon as I dropped this gear off my back. A cigarette, and a steaming hot cup of coffee. Heaven on earth. Meanwhile, the rain was coming down so thick we couldn't see an inch ahead of us. We were soaked to our very core, but had a spring in our steps: this would all be over soon. We could see the truck's headlights in the distance, and picked up the pace.

Just as we were about to reach the truck, our squad commander intercepted us. Without any introductions or explanations, he said: "You have another assignment. Head straight to Tel-Nof, where you'll be watching the airstrip. Tomorrow you infiltrate the base, place explosives on the airplanes, and then make your way to Hulda. You have half an hour to learn your assignment, fill up some water, and prepare the dummy-explosives."

We stared at him dumbfounded. Can't he see the condition we're in? Doesn't he understand we are running on empty? Does he not see the weather? Panic slowly gave way to anger. When we finally realized he was serious, we were filled with the deepest, most vile hatred towards him. I won't give him the satisfaction of seeing me break, I thought to myself. We went over to the truck, studied our axis of advance, prepped our gear, and were out of there in 20 minutes. The others took their time, but we were purposeful and incisive.

We started walking while the rain came down in buckets. We couldn't see a damned thing. We went along the train tracks like blind beggars, tripping over every rock and mound. We fell, and we got up, moving forward on nothing but sheer willpower. The wind was blowing straight in our face and we had to push hard just to keep moving forward. And then hail started falling. We were under attack by a relentless barrage of golf ball-sized hail, battering our faces and pounding our heads. We kept inching our way forward. We could barely breathe, it was raining so hard it felt like we were being waterboarded. Our feet, hands, and faces became completely numb. Hell was taking form and hitting us with everything it had.

We were supposed to follow the train tracks for seven miles, but didn't have the slightest idea how far we'd gotten. When it felt things couldn't possibly get any worse, the rain picked up to such a degree that we were literally knocked off our feet. We struggled to get up, and were battered right back down. We grabbed each other like two ants struggling to lift a veritable mountain of equipment.

Suddenly we spotted a small tin shack. We bumbled over to it, threw the door open, and rushed inside. We dropped to the ground panting like dogs, trying desperately to catch our breaths. After a couple of minutes, our eyes adjusted to the darkness, and we spotted two other people in the shack lying in bunk beds, too scared to move a muscle.

"Who are you?" I asked.

"Workers…" they said with a heavy Arab accent.

We all sat there in a nervous silence for a few moments, until one of them cautiously asked: "A-are you military? Soldiers?"

"Shut up! Don't ask any questions," I barked.

Silence fell again.

"D'you have a cigarette?" I half-asked, half-ordered. One of them handed me a cigarette and lit a match for me. The water droplets falling from my hair soaked the cigarette, but I took in the moist smoke with sheer delight. I hadn't smoked in four days. We sat there for ten more minutes in silence, feeling dozy in the cover and warmth of the shack. Finally, we shook ourselves off, grudgingly rose to our feet, and stepped back out into the storm, leaving the two stunned workers to ask themselves what the hell had just happened. Stopping for cover in the shack was against the rules, but we were way beyond the rules by that point.

We kept walking for I don't know how long, until we came across a road. We walked by the side of the road; we could just as easily have walked on the road itself, no one would spot us in that weather, but old habits die hard. We were supposed to stop at dawn, but we didn't. We carried on in a stupor of exhaustion. Our rain-soaked gear weighed well over 220 pounds, it felt like my machine gun was going to rip my neck off, and my feet were an utter mess of mud, blood, and rainwater.

At 6 AM we passed by the main bus station at Tel-Nof Base. Two soldiers were standing there waiting with umbrellas and raincoats on. They looked at us, appalled, two miserable-looking, ragged, mud-covered saps with gigantic backpacks dripping murky, brownish water.

"My mother was right," one said to the other, "she warned me not to volunteer."

We had a slight chuckle at his shrewd observation. We carried on in slightly better spirits, although that could also have been down to the fact the rain had died down a bit. We climbed up the hill overlooking the military airstrip. It was a great lookout point, full of shrubberies and precipitous cliffs – any soldier's dream. We knew we weren't allowed to go into caves because of the risk of catching cave-fever, but we found a shallow cave and convinced ourselves it was just a negative incline.[2] The afternoon was relatively dry, so I took the opportunity to take off my shoes and see what was going on in there. My feet were in horrible condition, covered in bloody blisters, the skin completely wrinkled from the constant moisture. I popped the blisters and drained them. I had a spare pair of socks, but they'd gotten wet along with

2 A negative incline is a cliff that creates natural cover, as the top of the cliff protrudes outward and over its base. It's a soldier's gag: "I didn't go into a cave, I found a negative incline." More often than not, it's a cave.

everything else in my backpack. I put them on anyway. I laced up my shoes as tight as I could. They were seriously worn out, and I prayed they'd last just one more night. They would not.

When night fell, we descended the hill and snuck up to the airstrip. We stashed our backpacks, skillfully disabled the electronic fence, passed by the guard dogs and crept towards the underground hangar. We pulled out small communications devices. Gilad kept watch while I snuck up to the planes. I placed the dummy-explosives in the first couple of planes, and looked beyond them. There was a lit room in the back, with the distinctive aroma of grilled-cheese sandwiches emanating from it. I could picture the toaster crisping the bread inside... I drew closer and closer, when all of a sudden the guard came out of the room. I could have just hidden in the shadows, but for some reason I became filled with a violent rage. I emerged from the shadows and stood right in his face. I looked him in the eyes and said quietly: "Go back inside, or I'll fucking kill you." He took one glance at me and bolted as fast as he could, slamming the door shut behind him.

We got out of there, found our gear, loaded it on our backs, crossed the road, and walked away as fast as our bodies could carry us. The rain picked up, pounding down as ruthlessly as it had the night before. We wallowed in the mud, hardly making any progress at all. We had to pass Soreq Stream, but it overflowed and flooded the fields around it. We lost our path. We went in a general direction, and it was all we could do not to fall into the raging waters. We were about 100 feet away from the train tracks. We could just about make out the embankment the track led to. Gilad was walking to my right, probably over whatever paved road was still left there. Suddenly I felt I was sinking.

I took one step and my leg sank knee-deep; I took another step, and my other leg sank down to the hip. I tried moving forward and quickly sank down to my waist. I pushed my torso down so that the weight on my back wouldn't drive me like a stake into the ground. It helped a bit, but then I started sinking forward. I knew that if I sank down to my chest, I'd be done for. I fought the mud, trying to swim across it like water. I shouted to Gilad at the top of my lungs, but he couldn't hear me over the deafening storm. I fought like a trapped animal to keep myself afloat. One minute I'd gain a few inches, the next I'd sink right back down.

Gilad had made it to the embankment. He turned around to look for me, but couldn't see me. I yelled out to him again, but he couldn't hear me. I kept struggling… I started swallowing mud. I tried turning to my side, but my backpack pulled me down like an anchor. In the course of my frantic struggle, I realized I had to spread out and make as large a surface as I could. I tried taking off my backpack, but sudden movements made me sink deeper. Gilad slumped to the ground to wait for me. I screamed with everything I had left in me – he turned around, but didn't see me.

I kept moving constantly, intuiting that if I stopped, I'd sink like a stone. I kept yelling, but to no avail. Just then, a fierce lightning bolt tore the sky apart; during that brief moment of light, Gilad spotted me. He threw his backpack aside and rushed over. I screamed for him to keep back. "What should I do?" he screamed back. "Rope! Throw me a rope!" I yelled. Gilad took out the rope from his vest while I struggled to unload my backpack. I kept wiggling constantly, to keep from sinking further. He tossed the rope, but it fell short. He pulled it back to try again. Meanwhile, I'd managed to get out of my backpack and hurl it forward with everything I had. The damned thing floated; must have had enough air trapped inside it. I took off my machine gun and tossed it over as well. I furiously tried to swim through the mud towards my gear, exerting every tiny bit of energy left in my body – but hardly made any progress. I desperately fought on, progressing inch by inch. The rain was incessant; strangely enough, I felt it actually helped by diluting the mud. After what seemed like forever, I made it to my backpack.

Gilad carefully approached from the other side. He tossed his rope again, but again fell short. I had to repeat the stunt with my pack and weapon, but this time I knew what I was doing. I relaxed for a second, immediately realizing that was a mistake as I sank deeper. I worked up a frenzy again, drawing energy from god-knows-where.

He tossed the rope for a third time, and this time it reached me. I latched the spring-hook at its end to my backpack, and Gilad dragged it out of the mud. We then repeated the drill with my machine gun. All the while, I kept stirring and shifting to keep from sinking further. As I slowly progressed, I felt the lace of my left shoe snap. I tried my best to salvage it, but quickly realized it was either me or the shoe. I gave up the shoe. Shortly after, I managed to make it to somewhat-solid ground and crawled on all fours, forcefully extracting my hands and legs from the mud with each step. Finally, I was able to make it to my feet. My heart was racing. My entire body was violently quaking from the exertion. Gilad later told me that I was screaming like an animal the whole time, occasionally laughing like a madman. I don't remember any of that.

Gilad dragged my gear up the embankment and I crawled on all fours. We sat there, huffing and panting. The rain was as relentless as ever. I started having massive cramps in every part of my body: my legs, my arms, my hips, my back… I wiggled around trying to ease the pain, feeling my muscles were going to tear off the bone. In a maddened burst of rage, I suddenly leaped to my feet and shook all my limbs.

"You can walk?" Gilad asked, stunned.

"Let's go! Now!" I screamed at him.

He helped me load my gear and we resumed following the tracks towards the road. I only had one shoe on, but couldn't feel my foot anyway. I started feeling lightheaded and cheerful. It was as if my head was filling up with oxygen and just casually floating, slowly drifting away from my body. We made it to the road. I felt the ground slipping from under my feet, and then everything went dark.

The next thing I felt was a tongue on my forehead… I was inside two sleeping bags stuffed with heat packs inside the lit truck. My squad commander was checking my temperature with his tongue.

Later, Gilad told me what happened – that he saw me drop like a sack in middle of the road and rushed over to me, checking to see that I still had a pulse. He tried to flag down a car to stop for us. The first one drove right by. When the second one approached, Gilad stood right in its path and pointed his rifle straight towards the driver. Gilad and the driver loaded me and my gear up to the car and drove to Hulda.

I woke up again on the bumpy road up to the unit. To my surprise, I was able to get out of the sleeping bags and stand up. The squad commander asked me how I was feeling, and I replied that I was fine. From there, I went straight for a long, steaming hot shower and a cigarette in bed. Tomorrow's a new day, I thought to myself, but how am I gonna explain to the quartermaster that I need a new shoe…

On Sunday, we headed out for a week-long series of land navigation.

CHAPTER 6

1,100 MAG ROUNDS: OPERATIONAL DUTY

Even before officially completing their training, combatants are desperate to join the fight. Operational duty is the culmination of everything you've studied and trained for, it is the ultimate test.

In March 1978, the invasion of South Lebanon – named "Operation Litany" – had begun, and no one took us into consideration. We were in the Negev Desert doing a navigation exercise, and the operation simply started without us. My commander, Nachum Lev, then still a young squad commander, was absolutely livid. We quickly hopped onto the D500 truck, and he ordered the driver to floor it back to the unit. When we got there, Nachum went to find himself a signaler, and we started prepping our equipment and gear.

A few months earlier, I'd inherited the MAG machine gun after my predecessor was discharged. The FN MAG is a large and heavy Belgian-made general-purpose machine gun, shooting 7.62mm rounds from heavy metal ammunition belts that are difficult to handle. But this doesn't even begin to describe the myth that surrounds this weapon. In every infantry unit, the MAG is a status symbol, a certificate of honor for its bearer. The machine gunner, or gunner in short, walks around with an aura of being the best and strongest among the soldiers in his company.

I went to get ammo. The unit's kennel had no dogs in it, but it had ammo – lots and lots of ammo. I took five crates of bullets and grabbed a couple of stray ammunition belts. It took me three rounds to carry all that to my room. Infantry units have a position called "MAG 2", an assistant gunner who is effectively the gunner's porter. But our unit is tight and compact, we had no room for assistants, so we just carried whatever we could ourselves. I initially stored the ammunition belts in drum magazines, which allow you to store rounds in a spiral around the center of the magazine – a nifty way to keep your ammo close to the gun. The problem is if the magazine jams. The only way to clear the jam is to tear the belt, but then all the other rounds in the drum become useless. So, on second thought, I left only one drum magazine, scattered the rest of the belts in the pockets of my combat vest, and shoved the rest into my backpack.

Finally, Nachum returned. We loaded the truck and were off to Lebanon, stopping for falafel in Afula along the way. The next morning, after a very short night's sleep at the border, we reached the town of Arnoun, overlooking Marjaayoun. We linked up with the Golani and Paratroopers Brigades' reconnaissance companies. They had already conquered al-Khiam and the entire Marjaayoun range. The bastards left nothing for us.

I went to look for Yoav, a childhood friend who served in the Golani reconnaissance company. I found him asleep, safe and snug in a one-piece snowsuit. He was happy to see me, and told me all about the battle they'd participated in the day before.

Finally, Nachum came back with an assignment, and the feeling of humiliation at once turned to eager anticipation. We were certain elite soldiers like us would be given the assignment to end all assignments, something to end this whole operation in one fell swoop. We would take enemy headquarters, destroy the very seat of evil. But instead, it turned out we were being sent to destroy a mortar position that was bugging the troops… Well, better than nothing, I guess. We were supposed to sneak up to the position at night, destroy it and the surrounding forces, and return to bask in our glory.

We gathered the night equipment. I managed to cram 650 rounds into my combat vest and drum magazine in different ways. My overall weight was heavy, but I believed I'd manage. I stuffed whatever was left into my backpack and looked for someone with room on their backs to carry it. There was no such person. Everyone had geared up from head to toe. It was our first time going out on operational duty, and no one wanted to be caught ill-prepared: mortar shells, rocket launchers, grenade launchers, RPGs... We were armed to the teeth, ready to stop a whole armored convoy if necessary—but no one had room on their backs.

We held roll call and Nachum examined us one by one.

"What about the pack?" he asked me.

"I'll carry it. I'm gonna empty all the ammo at the destination, anyway."

Nachum lifted the backpack, hardly looking up at me. "Are you sure?" he asked. "You're walking lead tonight."

I gulped, and replied that I was sure. At night, the commander leads the team, walking the most direct path to the target. Whoever leads to his right or left maintains his line at a fixed distance, no matter the terrain, no matter what obstacles are in the way. The gunner usually doesn't lead, but in cases where direct enemy fire is anticipated, it's best to have your superior firepower leading the line.

I loaded the heavy pack on my back. I was carrying 1,100 MAG rounds, a combat vest and gear, water canteens, grenades, a combat knife, and other miscellaneous combat gear. All in all, over 155 pounds. The first steps were nearly impossible. Once again, I felt like I was being driven into the ground with each step. When we fell into formation and I knelt by a thorn-bush on the side of the path, I could barely get myself back up to my feet.

When we departed, just walking was nothing short of a nightmare. I awkwardly plowed my way through the vegetation like a tank, occasionally having to run forward to catch up with Nachum. Running with all that weight on my back required the coordination of every single muscle in my body.

I huffed and puffed like a dying engine. That bulky machine gun slung over my neck nearly toppled me over with every step I took. My back muscles screamed, my leg muscles became stiff and swollen. I kept moving and running to keep up. One thought played in my head obsessively: As soon as we make contact with the enemy, I'm blasting every single goddamned round I'm carrying. When we stopped, I didn't kneel out of fear I wouldn't be able to stand back up. In the meantime, every stone along the way posed an impenetrable barrier, any incline was like climbing the Everest.

After about three hours, when I was certain I had absolutely walked my last step and was about to collapse in exhaustion, Nachum stopped and whispered the magic words: "Staging position." I thought this moment would never come. Nachum signaled me to scale a nearby mound. I took off my pack, positioned the MAG and spread some ammunition belts. Three of us were left behind to provide cover fire, while Nachum and the rest of the team set off to outflank the mortar position. Once I received the signal, I would fire the longest burst any gunner ever fired. Then I intended to move the barrel and just pound away, shooting at anyone and anything that tried to flee the scene.

I dripped sweat all over the MAG, constantly having to wipe my sweaty palms. Time went on, but no signal came. Another fifteen minutes passed, nada. Finally, I stopped sweating, but now I was getting cold. After another fifteen minutes or so, Nachum and the team emerged from the darkness and signaled us to fall in. There had been no mortar, nor was there an enemy... The place turned out to have been deserted.

I packed everything up and we started heading back. Words cannot describe the agony of the way back: I was beyond pain and despair. I cursed the terrorists who refused to stay in one place, I cursed Nachum who first suggested I would regret how heavy my pack was, I cursed the guy who left the team and bequeathed me this accursed machine gun, and I cursed the fact I couldn't just ditch the ammo and be done with it... In short, I cursed everyone and everything. A growl of fury and indignation was building in my chest the whole way back, threatening to make its way up my throat and burst out. It was this pent-up rage that drove me forward on that long, arduous walk back.

When we finally reached the starting point, I threw off my pack and took off my combat vest. I was soaking wet, as if I had just stepped out of the pool. I steadied the MAG on its bipod, and went to look for a cigarette.

CHAPTER 7

THE OUTSIDER: OFFICER TRAINING

At the end of the 18-month Qualification Course, the unit selects those who will become future squad commanders. It is a consequential decision for both parties, with significant ramifications to the lives of future cadets and their commanding officers.

I sat in the office of Tamir, the unit commander, alongside my squad commander Nachum, and I couldn't believe what I was hearing. An officer? Me? A squad commander? I can't say it came as a total shock, but still, I was surprised and honored. Tamir had taken his position as unit commander only a few weeks before, so I hardly knew him. He asked with a certain degree of apprehension if I wanted to be a squad commander, and I—excited as I was— completely neglected to play my role in this charade and immediately said yes. I was supposed to say no, insist that I just wanted to be a soldier in a team, and to let them convince me. That was how this was usually done, and that was what the two candidates in Tamir's office before me had said. But I, the city-slicker, the outsider, said yes right away. I didn't just agree, I was positively glowing. Tamir realized the guy sitting in front of him didn't quite fit into the usual mold here, just like him. He sighed with relief and struck up a casual conversation. Truth is, I was so excited that I didn't follow a word he was saying. Come to think of it now, I realize that out of the three people who participated in that conversation, I'm the only one still alive. Both of them died in the 90's. Tamir died in a helicopter accident trying to land in foggy weather; and Nachum was also involved in a helicopter accident which he actually survived, only to later be killed in a motorcycle accident.

The conversation was odd. Tamir was the kind of person who seemed out of place no matter where he was. He had come into the role following a legendary and admired predecessor. He had also committed an irredeemable sin: he was a paratrooper. Not that being a paratrooper was bad in itself, but this unit markedly preferred its own to outsiders. He was in good company, though; both Nachum and I were different from the other soldiers in the unit. Nachum was as talented as any other officer in the unit, but while most officers were kibbutzniks, raised in collective, secular communities, he was the son of a renowned religious scholar— although Nachum himself had left the faith and become secular. I myself was the only soldier in my squad to come from an urban background, the rest were also kibbutzniks; I was an aggressive guy among a group of level-headed lads; I was the only one in my squad who smoked, but I was in tremendous physical shape—a fact that drove the others mad; I was reading science fiction, they were reading belles-lettres or adventure novels; I had siblings and parents, they had the collective children's house; I didn't know any of the unit's alumni, they knew several from their kibbutzim; I didn't know any of the songs they sang around the campfire; they knew how to light a fire, navigate, walk in the dark, and get along in a group, while I had to learn all that from scratch. So how was it that while they were outside training, I was the one sitting in the unit commander's office?

I had always been the odd man out. I'd been an Ashkenazi boy in an almost entirely Mizrahi class. Even worse: I'd been a pretty boy with bright blue eyes. I'd had to fight for my spot. Of course, when I moved to the predominantly Ashkenazi elitist high school, I was considered "the kid from the slums." Even in my own house I was different, a lazy student sandwiched between a highly-accomplished older sister and a gifted younger brother. I studied only when I absolutely had to. Learning disabilities were unheard of back then, so they just said I was bright but recalcitrant. All my friends were non-Ashkenazis, and I preferred dark-skinned girls. Over time, I grew quite fond of the outsider's role, and honed my character to perfection. I wasn't afraid to be different, and made no great effort to fit in. I learned that one can be different and still fit in. I was part a group of friends, but at the same time I was always a maverick: I believed in friendship, but even more, I believed in being true to yourself.

In the army, the cultural differences between myself and the kibbutzniks were staggering. I tried to understand what they were about; I even went over to their kibbutzim on several weekends. But I didn't relate to what I saw, and even though I made an effort to understand them, I never wanted to be like them. And because I never tried to fit into their mold, I became an alternative type of leader in the unit. Some of them even came over to my "camp," so to speak; but at the end of the day, none of those friendships lasted to the present.

Being nominated for officer training fit my own perception of myself, but I was surprised to discover how hard it actually proved to be. In the unit, we were trained in every aspect of commando warfare: land navigation, night raids, camouflage, single or small-group combat, etc. But I didn't know the first thing about infantry warfare, and when we had our first infantry exercise— to take an enemy-held fortification— I was like a fish out of water. Things went from bad to worse as the battlefield maneuvers grew in scale and became increasingly complex. I just couldn't wrap my mind around the idea of two opposing forces duking it out face-to-face in an open battlefield. Such a scenario requires a holistic perception of the battlefield as a whole and exact coordination and division of targets and objectives, requiring a level of cooperation to which I—a commando brought up in inherently small, tight-knit teams—found it hard to acclimatize. However, when it came to individual soldiery, I stood out: after several navigation exercises which I finished hours ahead of anyone else— one time even reaching the end point before the truck that was supposed to mark it— I was excused from navigation training. I stood out physically, although there were some individuals who were faster than me, and one or two who were as strong as I was. But when it came to the "Natural Disaster" exercise, in which we had to run over sand dunes, run in the sea, climb up a cliff, pass an obstacle course, and then shoot at targets— I received the highest score of anyone in the course.

Yet I took to heart the gulf in knowledge between

myself and others regarding broader frameworks of warfare. Try as I might, I couldn't make up the ground, and gradually slumped into a let's get this over with mood. I made friends there whom I held in high esteem, especially those who excelled in places where I struggled. And eventually it was over. My squad, who just so happened to be doing a navigation exercise nearby, were able to attend the graduation ceremony. Seeing their delightfully uncouth support in the stands went a long way to brightening my mood as I stomped around the parade ground.

When we got back to the unit, I once again found myself neither here nor there. I had agreed in advance to extend my service by three additional years, and thus I was earmarked to lead the next squad available. Until then, I had several months as a free agent in the unit. I went on every operation, honed every skill I desired, but I felt unsatisfied—I wanted my own squad already.

Finally, conditions were such that I was able to get a team of newly-arrived cadets. I jumped at the chance. The make-up of this squad was completely different than all other squads: it had a city majority, and only a tiny minority of kibbutzniks and the odd cadet from an agricultural settlement. That suited me very well—fewer smartasses, more practicality. Plus their group consciousness wasn't as developed, meaning they would be easier to shape in my image.

I adopted a primus inter pares approach as a commander, opting for sociability over distance. Whatever they did, I did too. I was better than them at most things, but as some of them grew to outperform me in certain aspects, I embraced it. Not that I ever stopped competing with them, but I could accept losing a 5-mile race, for example.

True to the belief that there's a wild, killer side in all of us that needs to be unearthed, I kept poking and prodding to awaken the beast in them. I wholeheartedly believed that in order to be a commando, you needed to be able to call on the killer in you at will. Living in a society regulated by social norms, we are forced to bury that side of us deep beneath the surface; you cannot be a normal, functional member of society if you don't learn to tame the ruthless impulses inside you. But when you push yourself close to the edge, you increase your chances of stirring the slumbering beast inside: when you fight in hand-to-hand combat, there will come a moment where if you are still restrained— you will lose. When you are out alone on assignment in the middle of the night in unfamiliar territory, all the cool thinking, skills, or knowledge you possess are worthless—if your killer instincts are not awake, you will be mired in fear and trepidation.

So I deployed the entire scope of training available to me in the unit, and devised a couple of exercises of my own. Two to three fitness sessions a day; monstrous ruck marches, some exceeding 30 miles in a single night; extensive hand-to-hand combat training, and no-holds-barred fights. I demanded aggression. I took them out drinking, because drinking helps remove inhibitions. I got them involved in street brawls. I demanded they perform even in the face of extreme deprivation.

In most cases, it worked. I discovered different people had different wild sides to them, and that some people had developed elaborate mechanisms to keep that wildness at bay. I also discovered that some were incapable of reining in that wildness once it was unleashed. So I trained them in that as well. This confrontational style had a price: most of them were injured at some point. Some recuperated and returned stronger, but some had to quit. This method also ran the risk that natural-ly-imbalanced people could get completely derailed and become sociopaths or criminals. So at the same time, I emphasized and promoted integrity, self-respect, re-spect for your peers, and— most importantly—loyalty. In my squad, Zionism was a framework through which to channel and focus violence and aggression.

At the end of the day, I got the squad I wanted: a team of warriors who could absolutely rip the enemy to shreds. A squad that could unleash unparalleled savagery, allowing them to do what others simply couldn't; at the same time, they could sit together moments later, console each other, and feel empathy and compassion. That team proved itself on many occasions. We had our failures, sure, but not once did they result from a lack of ability.

CHAPTER 8

INDEPENDENCE DAY 1980: RECKLESS ABANDON

Defying conventions. A clash of two worlds.

As Independence Day approached, we finished roll call and prepared for a dull, routine stay at the base over the holiday. We were the on-call anti-terror team on the base. So we readied our gear and prepared to loaf around meaninglessly.

To my surprise, I was summoned to the unit commander's office. I was instructed to tell my team to put on their formal uniforms and head over to secure the official state ceremony at Army Headquarters in Tel-Aviv. It was a far cry from what we were used to doing, but an order is an order. Plus there would probably be some good food there.

I inspected my soldiers thoroughly before our

departure. I sent them to fix whatever needed fixing and borrow whatever they were missing in order to have their formal attire comply with regulations. Some, who hadn't yet shaken off the stench of a week out in the field, I even sent to shower. Finally, we were ready. We had several different weapons, each serving a different purpose, but each of us had a favorite weapon we preferred to carry in formal settings. Mine, unlike the rest of the team's, was a shorter and lighter refitted M16 assault rifle, an Israeli renovation which was relatively new at the time. We were given four new and shiny jeeps, so we could make a fitting entrance.

We arrived at Army Headquarters with the arrogance and pomp that reflected our prestige. I presented myself to the head of security, who immediately sent me to see the base commander. The event was held outdoors in a finely-decorated garden. The base commander walked around as proud as a groom on his wedding day. I was surprised to discover that I recognized him: he was a close friend of the family. I'd had no idea he was a base commander… As soon as he noticed me, he instructed me to stay by his side the whole evening. I asked that my soldiers be taken care of, and he had them posted by the buffet. I went over and warned them to behave themselves.

We all remembered far too well the last time we

stayed at a different base and I asked them to behave themselves. It had been the Tel-Nof air force base, where the army parachuting course was held. We were there to exercise loading and unloading a jeep from a helicopter. In the break between day practice and night practice, I sent them to grab lunch at one of the base's mess halls. I myself went to look for a friend I knew was stationed there. I was just about to meet up with her when I suddenly heard a commotion. I rushed over to the scene and saw that my worst fears had been realized: the soldiers had decided to eat at the most sacred of places in the base—the parachuting instructors' mess hall. In line for the food, egos on both sides had flared up. My men were clutching the helmets they were using in practice, so it wasn't exactly a fair fight... Long story short, by the time I reached the place, one soldier was under arrest and the rest were expelled from the base. It took me 48 hours to get Eitan out of detainment, and even that was only due to the fact that we were going out on a covert operation that couldn't be postponed. As for the parachuting instructor, well, I think it took him more than 48 hours to be discharged from the hospital with a fractured skull...

The party was gathering pace. The security forces and the government's corps d'elite were all there in their finest clothes: high-ranking officers and their wives, senior members of the Ministry of Defense, high-profile civilian contractors, etc. At first, I obeyed the base commander's order and followed him around; he enjoyed parading me to his colleagues, but none of them had anything to say to me. Pretty soon, I realized he was growing a bit uncomfortable having me around him: I was at least a foot taller than he was, lean and muscular, and much younger than him. When someone pulled him aside to whisper something in his ear, I seized the chance and got out of there. I found a bar table far from the action, lit a cigarette, and sat down to observe the guests.

"Do you have a spare one for me?" she asked.

I turned around. She was incredible, sexy in every sense of the word. She was tall with curled hair and sensual lips, full luscious breasts, a tight waist and long legs, all squeezed into a tight, deeply-cut, split-side black dress. She was older than me by at least ten years, and way out of my league.

"Cat got your tongue?" she asked teasingly. "Actually, it's quite endearing that you're embarrassed. What's the matter, honey, you've never been hit on?"

"Well, not by someone like you," I said, and even managed to smile.

"So what about that cigarette, then?" she asked. There was a smile in her eyes, and she suddenly looked much younger.

I rifled through my pants pocket, pulled out a pack of cigarettes and offered her one. I lit it using a combat Zippo lighter that I never took out into the field. She examined the lighter with interest. It was adorned with some sort of complex military insignia.

"What is it? Something secret?"

"Very."

"Oh, well, in that case you'd better hold on to it," she said, and playfully smiled again.

My eyes kept drifting to her cleavage, which captivating.

"My eyes are up here, you know," she giggled and pointed at her eyes.

"I'm sorry, they're amazing… I-I mean, you're amazing."

"You haven't seen the half of it," she said and leaned into me. Her bouncy breasts pressed against my shoulders, and I could feel my heart racing.

"Don't tell me you're a virgin."

"Not quite…" I managed to mutter.

"Too bad, I like virgins. They're very… eager."

"Not too eager?"

"There's no such thing, honey," she winked at me.

Two of my soldiers came over to ask me if I needed something. They never called me sir, and usually never addressed me without reason. It was clear they just wanted to get a closer look at her, and perhaps help me by making me look important. I brushed them off with a flick of my wrist.

She grazed the barrel of the rifle slung over my shoulder with her fingernail.

"You're a dangerous man."

"You have no idea how dangerous."

"And you're brave."

"The bravest."

"Good. You'll need to be, soon," she said, as a tall man in a suit approached us. He was handsome and older than she was, a self-confident man who exuded success.

"Look who I ran into," she said and squeezed my bicep firmly. "You remember Wexler's boy, right?"

He had a confused look in his eyes for a moment, but quickly gathered his wits: "Sure, of course I do," he said and shook my hand firmly. "How are you? How are your parents?"

"They're fine," I said, wondering what the hell was going on. I've been called many names before, but Wexler was never one of them. I was astounded by her audacity.

"Are you coming?" he turned to her. "It was nice to see you," he said, turning back to face me, "send my regards to your parents."

She stroked and pinched my bottom as she walked away.

I was left standing there, completely stunned. What

just happened? This was an operational opportunity, and I did not strive to make combat contact.

I wandered around aimlessly. I approached my soldiers; they teased me about the encounter, which they had observed with attention. They were busy eating, and I warned them not to drink any alcohol. I left them there and kept on wandering.

Suddenly I saw her strutting her way to the restroom. I followed her and waited for her at the exit. The restroom door swung open, she grabbed me by the arm and pulled me in. Before I could understand what was going on, she squeezed into me and kissed me strongly, hungrily, arms tight around me. Her tongue explored my mouth as she grabbed my hand and placed it on her breasts. I became impassioned. I forcefully kneaded her breasts with one hand, feeling her perky nipple through the thin fabric of her dress, squeezing her buttocks with my other hand, feeling her feminine curves. I pulled her in close, her body wriggling against me… Without warning, she suddenly pulled away from me. She looked me in the eyes, panting. She opened the door and pushed me out.

I stood there smiling like an idiot. She came out a couple of minutes later, stuffed a note into my palm, and teasingly strutted away. Scribbled in red lipstick, the note read: Liat, tomorrow, 34 Ben-Yehuda St., 4th floor, 4 o'clock.

The next day, I asked one of the other squad-commanders to come in and replace me. I took a jeep and hightailed it to Tel-Aviv. At a quarter to four, I rushed up the flight of stairs to the fourth floor of an old apartment building on Ben-Yehuda street. As I stood there trying to decide which of the three doors in front of me to knock on, one of them opened. There she was, her nipples protruding from the skimpy sheer dress she wore. I came in and closed the door behind me. It was a studio apartment and we were the only ones there. She smiled mischievously.

"Take off your shirt," she whispered. I did, and threw it aside. She reached out and stroked my chest.

"You're strong," she said. "Will I have to wait much longer for you to pounce on me?"

I clutched her dress in my hands and tore it forcefully, her beautiful breasts bursting out. I grabbed both of them, delighting in their luscious firmness. I bent down to kiss her erect nipples, mouthing one and then the other. I tore her dress further until it slumped down to her ankles, revealing her body in its entirety. With nothing on but a tiny black thong, she jumped on me, her legs coiling around my waist. We bumbled our way over to the bed; I ripped her underwear off, and she purred like a kitten. An hour later, we lay exhausted in her bed.

"You smell nice," she said as she stroked my arm.

"So do you."

"And you taste nice," she said, and bit me— stirring a second round of tumultuous love-making.

That afternoon, I found out that she was married, that she had two girls— Neta and Michal— and that she loved her husband. I also learned that the apartment belonged to her friend, and that she never wanted to see me again because I was nothing but a fling.

The next day, she called the unit. Any call to the unit first reached an operator who transferred the call if they knew where you were; otherwise, they'd announce your name over the PA system. That way, everyone always knew who was calling whom and how frequently.

She said she missed me, and that she hadn't meant it yesterday when she told me she didn't want to see me again. I told her I was busy, that I was going out, and that I wouldn't be available. She insisted and asked me when I would be available, and I replied: "Sometime in the future…"

I held out for a week. We met again for a particularly wild evening. It then became a habit: once every couple of days we'd meet— in a hotel room, in a friend's apartment, at the beach, etc. When I wasn't with her, I swore to myself I'd never see her again. But then she would call, and I would make up an excuse to leave the base to go see her. When I was out in the field, I felt torn between two opposing forces: an irresistible attraction versus the rational understanding that this relationship wasn't good for either of us.

Meanwhile, our rendezvous became more and more feverish. We made love at the beach, in public parks, in an army jeep, in the car under her house, by the entrance gate just outside of the base... We pursued our passion with reckless abandon.

One time, I was conducting an urban navigation exercise for my team. They learned the axes of advance, and in the evening, we took an army truck out to a parking lot in southern Tel-Aviv. They hopped off in civilian clothes and with concealed weapons, and started the exercise. I told the driver he could go off and do as he pleased, while I hung around waiting. A short while after, just as we scheduled, a silver Audi pulled up to the truck. She stepped out, catlike and sexy, and climbed into the cabin. The smell of the army truck turned her on: she pounced on me, pinned me down, and tormented the hell out of me. We were so engrossed in ourselves we didn't notice the time. When I finally snapped back to reality, I noticed some soldiers had completed the exercise and were huddled not far from the truck. I was nervous. Liat smiled, straightened her dress, opened the door and stepped out of the truck, strutting her way towards her silver Audi. The soldiers gaped at her, dumbstruck. She blew me a kiss, got in the car, and drove away. I dug my heels in and refused to answer any of their questions…

The next time I saw her, silence was no longer an option. I was having a couple of beers with my soldiers in the Tavern pub behind the Exhibition Grounds in Tel-Aviv. Suddenly I could smell her perfume. She placed her hand on my shoulder and squeezed in between me and the soldier sitting next to me. She was there with a friend. She chatted briskly and lightly with the soldiers, spreading obvious hints about the nature of our relationship. Later, she pulled me into the bushes, making sure that everyone could see where we went.

Our relationship became the most well-known secret in the unit. The soldiers did what they could to cover for me, even when I pushed the boundaries of acceptable behavior. What did they think of their commander? I didn't know, and didn't ask. They occasionally asked me about her, clearly taking pleasure in embarrassing me.

The whole time, I kept reminding her that she had a lot to lose; that she had a family she loved, that her life was good, and that she didn't need me. She always agreed with me, but would then call me and we'd meet up again.

Until she finally stopped calling. A week passed, followed by another, and then another… A month later,

I called her myself. Her husband answered. He let me speak with her, and must have been standing next to her. She told me she didn't want to see me again, that she'd told her husband everything, and that she'd promised him it was over. I didn't know what to say. I said good-bye, and hung up the phone.

A couple of days later, she called. She said she hadn't meant any of what she said, that it was all an act for her husband. I replied that I understood, but that it really was wrong. We agreed we wouldn't see each other any-more. That resolution lasted about a month, and then we met again and absolutely ravaged each other. And just like that, it was back to square one.

One day, I was called in for a conversation with Tamir, the unit commander. It was pretty unusual, but I wasn't too bothered. He was a good commander, appreciated and respected by everyone in the unit.

To my surprise, he started talking about his family, about his kids and his special bond with them, and about the importance of the family cell in his life, which gave him the strength to perform his professional duties well. I sat there awkwardly, not sure what was going on. He then said that the family cell was important for every-one, and that one thing a man with honor never did was ruin a family.

I stared at him, flabbergasted. "You're having an affair

with the wife of a close friend of mine," he said. "I'm sure you like her, but think of the damage you're causing. I'm not asking you to do anything, and I'm not ordering you either. Make your own call."

I was left stunned. I never called her again, and I turned away all her calls. Slowly, they became less and less frequent, and finally stopped altogether. It would be many years before I heard of her again.

CHAPTER 9

TEAM ASSIGNMENTS: GRIT AND ARROGANCE

The hardest tests are the ones you put your own self through.

Back in my day, there was no training course for squad commanders. What you yourself underwent as a cadet during the qualification course served as your training. You were offered tools and assistance when you sought them, but at the end of the day it was down to you to conceive, plan, and execute your own ideas. Near the end of the qualification course, there is a time slot reserved for "team assignments." Team assignments comprise a weeklong "rolling" exercise, during which the cadets execute nightly assignments drawn from the arsenal of operational scenarios they have mastered. The daytime in between is spent hiding in team-camouflage (requiring a great deal more skill and equipment than individual camouflage), meaning you carry a mass of gear, equipment, and provisions along with you. I didn't know it then, but the events that would unfold during team assignment week would play a decisive role in forging my team's identity. By the time the exercise was finished, it would become known to everyone that we were a wild, daring, and resolute group, with exceptional operational capabilities.

The only problem was that I hadn't taken part in team assignment week during my own training; it had been conducted after we completed our qualification course, and I was already in officer training by then. Usually, you'd look to what your own squad commander did when drawing your own plans. I first turned to my company commander, but he was new and hadn't done it himself either. I had no choice but to turn to my old squad commander, the legendary Nachum Lev. I was reluctant to call on Nachum— you don't want to ask your squad commander for help, you want to prove to him you're good enough on your own. But Nachum, as ever, was practical and incisive.

"Start with silent infiltration into some kind of security complex, then a live fire raid on some target, and finish up with storming a military base. In between, make sure you practice camouflaging in different terrains, and add some retreat exercises with loaded stretchers." He had the same sparkle in his eye when instructing me now as he had when I was his cadet. "And make sure to throw in vehicle abduction at some point, to help you cover some ground…" he concluded with a typical wink.

I went to speak to the operations officer, to see what options I had. I concocted an exercise. I took a jeep and rode around alone for three days to scour the target areas. I then presented my plan to the unit commander. He was not impressed, and told me to come up with a better plan. I consulted David, an operations officer who was part of my old team before suffering an injury that forced him to take up a non-combatant role in the unit. Together, we were able to whip up a plan that won the approval of the unit commander, despite his displeasure at its loose ends. I was just happy to finally get his approval. I figured I'd just play the rest by ear as the exercise unfolded.

I checked the forecast on Friday and was dismayed to learn we were in for rain— an infantry soldier's worst enemy. Once again, those pesky showers that soak you to the bone, weigh you down with extra water weight, make you utterly miserable, and bring you to the verge of freezing. I couldn't add any extra gear to protect us from the cold, our backpacks were already filled to the brim; and besides, that wasn't how we did it in the unit.

We were expected to train with minimal gear. Nevertheless, I decided to allow every soldier to carry a thin nylon poncho.

After a full day of briefing and preparations, we held a gear-inspection roll call on Saturday evening. Every soldier lay their gear out on their beds, and I inspected them one by one.

"You don't need that."

"But…"

"No buts, there's no room for it. You need more ammo for the MAG."

"But I don't have any more space."

"Pass this to Amir, he has some space left and he's strong," I moved on to the next one.

"That's too much food, throw half of it away."

"It's a shame to throw food away…"

"Then eat it now."

After roll call was over, we made final preparations, last attempts to reshuffle the gear between packs, discarding some gear we might regret leaving behind. The soldiers helped each other load their gorged packs onto their backs, we hopped on the truck, and were on our way.

We reached our starting point. The soldiers quickly unloaded the truck, took off their winter coats, and loaded their packs on their backs again. There's a moment right before you step out of the warm truck when you are confronted with a clash between despair and motivation. But once that moment passes, you are filled with a mad desire to get started. Rain was drizzling, but it was nothing more than a slight nuisance; once we started walking, though, the floodgates opened and the rain came pouring down. But we were already in our stride and didn't mind getting wet.

Once we reached our destination, we stashed our packs, split into small squads, and went off on our first assignment. The rain came in handy here. There wasn't a soul to be seen out during such a storm, and the electric fence was going haywire because of the rain, allowing us to easily slip in undetected. We quickly stole the information we were assigned to obtain, and were out of there in a flash.

We got back to our packs, regrouped, and started snaking our way down the Carmel mountains. The soil was muddy from the incessant rain, and we constantly slipped over the wet rocks. The increasingly heavy packs made it difficult for us to get back up onto our feet.

Just before dawn, we found cover and camouflaged ourselves in some shrubbery overlooking the road to Yokne'am. We wrapped ourselves in our ponchos and tried to get some sleep. We were exhausted, but the cold was relentless and the shivering prevented us from sleeping. The rain stopped when day broke, and a nice winter sun emerged. We finally got some rest and gathered our strength for the night to come.

At last light, we packed our stuff and started moving. We ran across the road and climbed the opposing ridge, a short but very steep incline. We practically ran across Menashe Forest. It was cold, but dry. We kept our water breaks short so we wouldn't lose body heat.

During one such break, Sharon came over to me and reported his arm had gone completely numb. I took most of his gear myself, and divided up the rest between the others. He continued the exercise carrying only his combat vest and rifle. He didn't get the feeling back in his arm until some weeks later... Luckily for him he did get it back eventually, because years later he would become a famous mountain climber.

After gobbling up 18 miles of ground, we reached our destination before daybreak— a series of caves not far for the Arab village of Zababdeh near Camp Bazak, the Golani Brigade's home base. We were supposed to conduct a simple live fire raid exercise. We reached our staging position, took off our packs, and loaded up all our ammo. We set off towards our target. I positioned the holding force and started off in a stealthy rightward flank. We stopped at an acute angle from the entrance to the caves. I took the radio handset from Jacob to give the holding force the command to open fire. But then Jacob urgently whispered: "There's somebody there…" I picked up my night-vision goggles and couldn't believe my eyes: sleeping bags and military equipment. A whole company of Golani soldiers were camping in there.

I delivered the message as quickly and sharply as I could: "Do not open fire! Under no circumstances are you to open fire! Disarm your weapons!" I led the force back. We unloaded our weapons, gathered our gear, and were off as quickly as we could go. The soldiers were clearly irked they didn't get to shoot off some ammo weight, but I shuddered at the thought of the disaster we'd just avoided. To this day, the soldiers of that company— who had camped in a cave without coordinating with the base— have no idea how close they'd teetered on the brink of death.

That day, we hid ourselves in the basement of an abandoned house. We were pleased to be somewhere warm, but we were even more elated to be somewhere dry. I didn't allow the soldiers to light a fire, but a partying atmosphere prevailed nonetheless. It felt unprofessional, but I didn't feel like being a killjoy.

We left the basement when it was dark out, a group of tattered soldiers with humungous water-soaked backpacks. We placed a roadblock on a side road not far from the entrance to a godforsaken village in the middle of the West Bank. We dressed up as Military Police, with the white armbands and peaked caps, and waited for a truck that was sent out from the unit. In the truck was an operations sergeant who was wise as to what was about to happen, and a driver who wasn't.

The truck arrived and we pulled it over. We played the game, speaking only in Arabic. The driver believed this was an attempted hijacking, and feverishly tried to roll up his window. We smashed the glass and pulled him out through the window. He desperately held onto the steering wheel as if it were life itself, so we had to beat him a bit to break his grip. We put a hood over his head and tossed him in the back. The soldiers mounted the truck. Regev, one of my soldiers, had exceptional driving skills, so he took the wheel and we hit the road. The soldiers in the back couldn't help themselves and kept up the act. The poor guy was certain he had been kidnapped. When the exercise was over, I was sternly reprimanded and my team was ordered to pay for the driver's broken glasses. I had an officer's salary, so I covered the bill. In retrospect, we were let off easily; had it been today, we would have been tossed in jail for such a stunt.

I found a packet of cigarettes in the glove compartment, which I sucked down readily. We weren't allowed to take cigarettes with us, but I enjoyed breaking the rules. Regev drove expertly, and within two hours we reached the vicinity of Jericho. I looked for our starting point on the road. Once I found it, we loaded our gear, got off the road, and disappeared into the darkness.

After an hour of brisk walking we arrived at a firing range for another live fire team exercise. This time the company commander was the controller, and we did our best to impress him. When we finished the exercise, we completed a quick retreat to where we had left our packs, loaded them up, and were about to head out—when the company commander announced we had a wounded soldier.

We cursed under our breaths, knowing exactly what that meant. We opened a stretcher and volunteered Adi, the lightest among the soldiers, to play wounded. Make no mistake, though— being on the stretcher when it's cold out is no free ride. For those on the bottom, however, the old standard issue backpacks— with a metal frame and protruding horns on top— made it impossible to carry the stretcher. So four soldiers took off their packs and carried the stretcher, while four others carried two packs. Each pack weighed about 90 pounds each, reaching over 130 pounds together with the combat vest and rifle, so those who carried two packs were carrying something like 220 pounds on their backs. We had to climb up to the hilltop fortress of Sartaba Alexandrium, a hefty challenge even with no weight on your back. The company commander walked behind us up the steep hill and left us at the top. As soon as he left, I "revived" Adi; he was delighted to put his pack back on and regain some body heat. Luckily for us, it wasn't raining. We were exhausted, but still had another 6 miles to go to reach our hideout. We were hungry, our bodies were scraped and bruised, our clothes were torn, we were dirty, stinky, and soaked in sweat.

I walked at a medium pace, just fast enough to keep us from freezing. My feet hurt like I was walking on a bed of coals. An hour later, it started raining again. We picked up the pace. At the end of the road, a 6-mile ascent up a steep incline, was tomorrow's target: Camp Katzif.

We bundled up in our ponchos and spread across the ravine. It was cold, and the rain was relentless. We still managed to get some sleep. During the day, I occasionally woke up to muscle pain and spasms, shook them off, and dozed off again.

When night fell, we crawled out of our burrows. Every muscle in our bodies was screaming in pain. We slowly mounted our gear and focused on getting out of the ravine. We looked up again: a 6-mile-long ascent, albeit on a proper road this time. Every time a car drove towards us, we'd quickly get out of the way. We could see practically all the way up the road, meaning we'd spot the headlights of a vehicle from miles away. In fact, one was making its way down towards us at that very moment.

The soldiers all looked at me, and I knew exactly what was on their minds. One of them eventually said: "It's a commando initiative."

"What better way to infiltrate a base than using one of their own vehicles?" another said.

I was sold. We set up a makeshift blockade, while the rest of the team hid by the side of the road. We waited for the vehicle to approach, and to make sure it stopped, I stood firmly in the middle of the road. Eitan and Amir stood at my sides.

The truck stopped in front of us, and the entire force stormed at once. We pulled the driver out of the cabin and interrogated him. It turns out he was sent to pick something up from another base. We made it clear we were hijacking him, and he laughed. I slapped him forcefully, and two other guys pinned him down.

"This may look like a joke to you, but we're not here to play games," I said.

Eitan grabbed him by the neck with his huge hand. "Got it?!" he snarled at him. The rest of the soldiers surrounded him threateningly. We were blackened with mud and ash, reeking of sweat, caked in mud and blood, desperate. He got the point.

The team split into small squads I'd designated beforehand, when it was still our intent to sneak in through the rear fence. We got on the truck, and I crouched in the cabin by the driver's legs, pistol in hand.

"I won't shoot you, but I won't hesitate to break your leg," I said sternly. He believed me.

He turned the truck around and made his way back up towards the base. He slowed down in the middle of the road. I hit him forcefully in the shin with the handle of my pistol. He screamed in pain, and I gestured for him to keep driving. We reached the gate. The guards wondered what he was doing back so soon. The driver mumbled something. I tapped him on the shin again, and his imagination sprang to life.

"I-I forgot my coat," he told the guards.

"You're wearing it."

"No, not this one. My raincoat."

"What do you need a raincoat for?" they wondered.

That was enough for us. Four soldiers jumped off the back of the truck, snuck up from behind and incapacitated the guards, covering their heads with hoods and zip-tying their hands behind their backs. The rest of the guys rushed to carry out their assignments. Within minutes, every important building in the base was rigged with dummy-explosives. The driver fled the truck, and Regev took his place behind the wheel. He put it in reverse and swiftly spun it around while we all tried to jump on, but he hit a huge boulder, grounding the truck. He called on his full repertoire of maneuvers, but try as he might, the truck was truly stuck.

I leaped off the truck. "Everybody off!" I screamed, "we're walking." We had to get out of there before a reinforcement squad of paratroopers arrived from the nearby base. The team unloaded the truck like wild animals. We formed a single line on the road and started running. We were in a tight spot— this part of the road was carved straight into the mountain, and we were boxed in between two high-rising stone walls. On the next stretch of road, things went from bad to worse: on one side was a natural stone wall, while the other was a precipitous drop. We ran with all our might; we ran on fumes, but ran nonetheless. I could see headlights down the road heading in our direction. We kept running in the dark, and the bright lights got closer and closer. Endless scenarios flashed through my head as I tried to plan for the inevitable ensuing confrontation, but just then, the stone wall to our right dropped off and gave way to a mild slope. I hurled myself down the slope and the soldiers followed suit. We dropped off the road just in the nick of time: seconds later, a truck came flying around the bend where we had just stood.

"We have a new member in our team," Amir said. It turned out a magnificent German Shepard had accompanied us out of the base, and trailed us all the way to the slope on the side of the road.

"He's a warrior. He knows true warriors when he sees them," I said, and even though it wasn't the best of jokes, we all burst out laughing.

I signaled to the team that we were moving out. We still had another assignment to complete that night. We were very pleased with ourselves, and our spirits couldn't have been any higher. The soldiers started cracking jokes, and the discipline we had so carefully maintained was starting to slip. I stopped the party; I informed one of the soldiers that he was wounded, and that the rest of the team would carry him on a stretcher. They laughed while carrying out my order. Nothing could faze them now.

We walked slowly, weighed down by the double packs and the stretcher, but we were way ahead of schedule anyway. After a couple of hours, we reached a hill overlooking the "Atarot" airfield. We descended the hill and snuck into the airfield. After quickly jumping the fence, we huddled our backpacks at the end of the runway, split into squads and took over the airfield.

The control tower, who'd been expecting us, seemed

amused by us and happily played along. We drank their coffee, and I bummed a cigarette off one of them. That was that. All we had to do was wait for the Hercules aircraft to land. We set up makeshift runway lights, to simulate a real-life scenario. The advancing plane asked the control tower to turn on the runway lights. I told them not to. The person in charge of the tower said: "You're taking this too far, buddy. This is a safety matter."

That sentence snapped me back to reality. I really was a little too deep into the exercise. But then again, had I not been, we would not have been able to pull off what we did that night.

The plane landed, and all of us— including the dog— hopped on. We lay strewn across the floor like sacks of potatoes. The flight engineer gestured for us to sit in the side-facing seats. We gestured him back that he could sit down himself if he liked. It's impossible to sit with your gear on. He tried to convince me, screaming over the harrowing noise of the engine. I turned my back to him, and he went to consult the pilot. The pilot summoned me to see him. I laboriously climbed into the cockpit with my combat vest and weapon on.

"So take off your equipment," he rationally said.

"We don't take our gear off until the assignment is finished," I said. "As far as I'm concerned, you can leave us here. We'll walk back. We've already walked over 200 miles, what's a few more." Eventually the pilot gave in, closed the ramp, and took off.

We landed in the military airstrip in Lod. We alighted the plane, and I announced the exercise was officially over. No one had any energy left to celebrate. We dragged ourselves, along with our canine companion, onto the truck that was waiting for us and headed back to the unit, to begin the arduous process of cleaning our gear and weapons. When that was finished, we had a steaming hot shower waiting for us, and the ultimate luxury: beds with blankets in a heated room.

The next day, a message came from Camp Katzif: "Okay, you got us, but please return the dog." We tried to resist, but we had no choice, really. We said goodbye to the dog, and went to prepare Friday roll call before going home for the weekend.

CHAPTER 10

RETURN TO OPERATIONAL DUTY

Twenty years later, following the tremendous loss he had suffered, Erez volunteered to reenlist to the army.

Neta stood in the renovated office she'd taken care to organize over the past week, and looked over the camp where she served. About 6 miles south of Nablus was an old camp which once served as an infantry school. Following the Israeli-Palestinian accords, the school was relocated and the camp was repurposed as division headquarters. Neta had recently finished officer training, and was stationed at the division. A month prior, she'd been informed that a new headquarters would be established to coordinate the division's special units, and she was appointed to serve as office manager. She had two secretaries, an intelligence officer, an operations sergeant, an administrator, and a driver. She had everyone but a commander. Every time she asked, she was told he'd be coming any day now. The days went by, and she did her best to collect all the information she thought might be relevant.

That day, she had grown so exasperated from waiting that she decided to ask for a transfer. She even thought of asking her dad to call on his connections in Central Command. Just when she finally made up her mind to make that call, she noticed a black Chevy pulling up in front of the office.

A tall man emerged from the car, with broad shoulders and a slight sway in his step, as if he were walking on the deck of a ship. He had salt-and-pepper hair and a short, untrimmed beard that looked like he had just grown it out. He came into the office, said hello without shaking any hands, and kept his answers short. "Erez," he said simply, and asked Neta to show him the materials she had gathered. He listened with a sealed expression as the excited intelligence officer briefed him, and didn't correct her when she got some places' names wrong.

He went about his business incisively. He asked questions, and he requested materials. He didn't give any orders, nor any grand speeches. He simply came to work. That afternoon, he asked to see the most-wanted list. The files followed the American system of personality identification playing cards, in which names and faces of wanted terrorists were printed on a deck of playing cards. He read the files thoroughly, occasionally taking notes. Suddenly Neta felt a chill in the room. She looked up at Erez; he was holding the profile of one terrorist, his jaw tightly clenched. His hands firmly clasped the file, and Neta could see his muscles tense up.

He sat there silently for a couple of minutes, before suddenly getting up and leaving the room without saying a word. Neta picked up the file he'd dropped to the floor, which read: "Ibrahim Nasser, jack of clubs, directed several cells responsible for carrying out suicide bombings in Israel, including the Tel-Aviv central bus station, a children's bus in Jerusalem, and an armed attack in the settlement of Tapuach." The file went on to list family members and potential hideouts around Nablus. Neta didn't understand what had stirred Erez so. Despite her curiosity, she didn't ask.

The camp was first built by the British, then turned over to the Jordanians before falling into Israeli hands following the Six Day War in 1967. Many of its structures stood empty, and some were old and dilapidated. The office they'd been assigned was housed in an old building that had already been renovated once, but now consisted only of the three offices which stood at their disposal. Erez settled into one of the empty rooms. He put an army cot in the corner, and lay a sleeping bag over the mattress. He dragged a metal cupboard in from one of the other rooms, to keep his clothes in. A single chair and a desk completed the room's sparse furnishing. There were showers and restrooms down the hall from the office.

Erez got up every morning at 6 AM and went for a jog around the base, followed by a fitness session including chin-ups, pushups, parallel bars, and sit-ups. He then took a shower and went to get breakfast in the mess hall. By 8 AM he was in his office, planning the day ahead. He would then call his driver and go on long drives to scour the sector. When he got back around noon, he went down to the range and practiced shooting for an hour. Chaim the driver told Neta that Erez was conducting combat drills and that his marksmanship was unbelievable.

"Not only does he hit the target every time, it's almost always perfect headshots. Except for when he tells me he's aiming for the legs. He lets me shoot, as well. He says I'm his bodyguard in the field," the driver proudly said.

Later during the day, Erez would settle into his office and conduct a work meeting with Neta, go over materials he'd gathered from the intelligence officer, set up and coordinate meetings, and see to his daily tasks.

He made sure to grab dinner every evening, especially

on days when he'd skipped lunch, which were quite frequent. He then retired to his room to rest and read books. At 8 PM, he would go on another jog and fitness session, get back, shower, and work into the small hours of the night.

He gathered information, planned operations, changed plans, and issued orders. But he mostly worked on his strange pet project: he had hung a large aerial map in the office, and gradually covered it with things like observation post findings, cellphone triangulations, paths and tracks, and other bits and pieces of information he extracted from the growing dossier of raw data he was gathering. Cryptic colored markings grew like vines; circles, arches, and arrows appeared, followed by seemingly arbitrary dates; he jotted down and scribbled out equations on the edges of the map, made corrections, and added letters and symbols Neta vaguely recalled from advanced algebra class.

She tried to sound him out about it occasionally, but all she got were vague answers riddled with statistical calculations. His conduct continued to be professional, even courteous at times— but never personal. Sometimes she wasn't sure if he even remembered her name. He definitely didn't remember the intelligence officer's name.

Finally, he added a table to the map. In the first

column were terrorists' names, represented by their corresponding card signs and numbers; the second column listed locations by their coordinates; the third column consisted of dates, several per row; and in the final column were percentages, ranging from 70 to 90.

He asked Neta to set up a meeting with the division commander. She told him she was having a hard time setting up such meetings. He got up, grabbed a couple of files, and made his way to the brigade commander's office. He returned two hours later, and told Neta she wouldn't be having any more problems setting up meetings.

Two days later, Erez left the base wearing a combat vest and carrying a weapon. As he was heading out, Neta asked him where he was going, but he just mumbled inaudibly under his breath. The next morning, he wasn't in the office or in his room. Chaim the driver reported that he hadn't seen him jogging that morning. By lunchtime, Neta was growing increasingly concerned. She decided to report the matter, but didn't know to whom. That evening, she saw the brigade commander at dinner, and rushed over to him before he left the mess hall. She asked if she could speak with him; he was a little surprised, but entertained her request like a man speaking with a pretty woman, rather than as a commander and his subordinate.

"Erez is gone," she said plainly.

The brigade commander furrowed his brow and asked: "What do you mean, gone? Went home? Didn't come into the office?"

"Put on a combat vest, grabbed a weapon, got on a jeep, and left last night," she replied.

The bridge commander became white as a ghost.

"How do you reach him?" he asked. She looked at him in confusion, and he became irritated.

"When he goes out, doesn't he leave his coordinates with command post?"

"I sometimes do it for him. Honestly, I don't think he knows command post's number."

"Where does he usually go?"

"I'm not sure, to the villages around the base, maybe."

"Alone?" he asked in disbelief.

"With his driver, I think," she hesitated.

"Tell me, do you not know about his mental state?" He raised his voice. "Do you not know that he just suffered a severe trauma? Why did you wait until now to say something?!" he exploded.

The brigade commander called over some of his officers and issued some orders. Officers began scattering and running around. The PA system called for certain soldiers and officers to take up their posts.

Neta felt there was nothing more she could do and

returned to the office. She sat there unnerved, unsure what exactly the brigade commander meant, but certain there was something dark lurking in Erez. What kind of trauma did he suffer? What did the brigade commander mean? she thought to herself.

At 10 PM, she heard a vehicle pull up. She rushed to the window, and saw Erez coming up the stairs, dirty and gloomy, clutching his rifle in his hand. He entered the office and slumped down heavily in his chair.

"Everyone's looking for you. I went to the brigade commander and he blew his top."

Erez stared at the map in silence.

"Did you update the table?" he asked.

"Just what you showed me. I still don't get how it works," she replied.

"Get me the briefing."

He went over the documents and instructed her to mark some things down, then stood back and looked at the big picture. "Well, it doesn't really change much," he muttered.

Erez took a piece of paper and started jotting down complex equations. Neta had realized by then that those were probability equations. He went up to the table and updated some of the markings.

"Is there anything to eat around here?" he asked, hunched over the map.

"Just tuna and bread," she replied. She went out and came back with two cans of tuna and a loaf of bread.

"Water," he said without looking up from his calculations.

Neta was enchanted by his levels of concentration.

"Erez... the brigade commander said something about a recent trauma... What happened?"

"My kids were killed in a suicide bombing," he said, his face still buried in his calculations.

Neta stared at him, flabbergasted, struggling to believe what she'd just heard, but slowly feeling like things were starting to make sense.

"And the person who directed this attack... The jack of clubs?"

"Ibrahim Nasser, yes," he answered.

Neta looked at the table. The nearest date for Ibrahim Nasser was three days away, and the number by his name was 72%— relatively low. The next date was the following day, marked as 84%. As she was examining the table, Erez got up, grabbed a black marker and crossed out the queen of hearts.

"Why'd you do that?"

"He's dead," Erez answered laconically. He grabbed the two cans of tuna and bread, his bottle of water, a map, and a copy of the table, and stuffed them into his bag.

"Wait, where are you going?" she asked.

"If anyone asks, I wasn't here. And if Eitan is looking for me, tell him to call off the search. I'll be back later," he said.

"Erez, don't go," she said and stood in his path. She suddenly realized she was dressed in nothing but shorts and a tank top. Erez looked at her like he was seeing her for the first time.

Neta hugged him. He stood there motionless, passively letting her hug him. He then raised his arms and embraced her tightly. When she let go, he turned around and left. A couple of minutes later, she heard his car pulling away.

She stayed there in the office, unsure if she should let command post or the brigade commander know Erez was gone again. She decided to delay the call, to give him time to get away. The following morning, she went to see the brigade commander. His secretary refused to let her in, but when Neta informed her she had information about Erez, she was told to go straight in.

The bridge commander listened in silence as Neta repeated Erez's message, and silently stared at her at length.

"Tell me, isn't your last name Schiller?" he asked.

"Yes," she said, "why do you ask?"

"You know I was a soldier in Erez's team, right?"

"No, actually, I didn't know that. What does that have to do with anything?"

"Is your mother named Liat?" he prodded on.

"Y-yes, how did you know that?" she asked, taken aback.

"Did you ever tell your mother who you work for?"

"I did, and she actually asked me a lot of questions I didn't know how to answer."

Eitan sat there motionless for another moment, then picked up the phone and called off the search.

"What's the connection between Erez and my mother?" Neta asked.

"They had a long affair, years ago," the brigade commander replied.

Neta's jaw dropped.

"A-am I his daughter?" she asked in trepidation.

"No, no, it wasn't that many years ago. You were about four years old then, I think."

The phone on Eitan's desk rang. Someone on the other side reported something.

Eitan hung up the call and asked Neta: "What exactly did Erez say he was doing?"

"He didn't say. Why? What happened?"

"One of our most-wanted terrorists was killed last night."

"The queen of hearts…" It dawned on her. "He crossed him off the list!"

"What list?"

"The statistical list Erez keeps in our office," she replied.

Eitan got up, and without saying another word the two of them headed over to Erez and Neta's office. He stood in front of the map and examined it closely.

"That son of a bitch, he's actually doing it. He's trying out his theory!"

Eitan called in some officers who copied the contents of the map. Before they left, he instructed Neta to let him know immediately if Erez contacted her again.

"I'm not going to help you hunt him down," she said.

"We're not going to hunt him down. We're going to keep him safe."

CHAPTER 11

CROSSING A RAGING STREAM: END OF QUALIFICATION COURSE

Every course, even the toughest, comes to an end eventually. In the unit, you don't get anything for free: soldiers "buy" their qualification with a final exercise that incorporates all of the incredible abilities they have accumulated.

Winter, late 1970s. My team neared the end of its qualification course, with only the final exercise remaining. I wasn't bothered by the stormy weather. On the contrary: I thought it would be a good test, confident that the training they had undergone already would allow them to take on the challenge without too much trouble.

The soldiers spent the weekend going over the axes of advance and resting up. I took a jeep and went to scout the area. I reached the Be'er Sheva river, a dry stream bed in the southern Negev Desert. That was where the soldiers would be walking during the exercise, crossing the Be'er Sheva river from north to south at several points. It was a week-long solo exercise.

The usually-dry river was flowing vigorously after the rains that had fallen throughout that week. I parked the jeep, took off my shoes, pants, and shirt, and tried to cross the stream. I was thigh-deep in water, but managed to cross to the other bank and back with relative ease. As I made my way back to the jeep wearing nothing but my underwear and a rifle slung over my shoulder, a vehicle with four soldiers arrived—Military Police. Apparently, they came to check what this weirdo was up to. I growled at them; it was enough to scare them off.

The exercise started off with solo navigation around the Patish river. The soldiers were each dropped off at a point in the middle of a sector without knowing where they were, and started making their way towards the designated finish line. It was pouring buckets that day. The soldiers had to carry out an assignment in a nearby base, and then cross the stream and head south.

At the entrance to the base, I met the squad commander of the other team, and he told me that he was going to play it safe and get the soldiers across in a car. We had a couple of hours until the soldiers were due to arrive. I drove over to the stream and took my shoes off— they were soaked, anyway— and crossed the river again. To my surprise, crossing was even easier this time.

I sat waiting in the jeep at a mandatory point my soldiers had to report to before crossing the stream. The driver informed me he could get the soldiers across, no problem.

On the one hand, we cared about the safety of the soldiers. But on the other, these were elite commandos, super-soldiers, who would potentially be facing far more trying circumstances in operational duty. If I let them off the hook because of a little rain, what kind of message would I be sending? Things get a bit rough, so we give up? I knew that in one week's time the team would be transferred to the operational company, and I wanted hardened soldiers. And besides, in all honesty— they'd already been through much worse.

By the time the first soldier arrived, I had made up my mind. He reported to me, and I sent him down to cross the stream. There were several different points where they could cross, and each soldier decided for himself. They reached the bank at different points: some teamed up and crossed together, other went alone. They were all heavily equipped, carrying their webbing, weapon, and backpack— all completely drenched. It turned out that the places I crossed were particularly shallow. Some of the soldiers, then, walked into a dangerous nightmare.

Yigal, who was rather short, found himself in the middle of the stream with the water up to his neck. He fought desperately until finally making it across. When he reached the opposite bank, he sat down shivering from the cold and strenuous effort, cursing me and everything that had led him to that moment. Adi lost his footing and was carried away downstream. He summoned every bit of willpower and experience he had and grabbed a stone, held on, and with tremendous effort managed to stand up and resist the flow. Inch by inch, he managed to get across to the other bank. Climbing over the slippery, muddy bank was a feat in itself, requiring him to crawl on all fours. Others made it over by securing each other. At one point, Amir fell and Jacob pulled him over to the bank.

I had no idea who'd made it across and how, since I only saw them much later, in the small hours of the night. I let out a heavy sigh of relief when the last of them arrived: soaked, covered in mud, spent and exhausted, but ready to continue.

The other team made it easily and safely across in their ride. Years later, my team would poke fun at them, calling them "dissolvable sugar soldiers." The other squad commander was upset with me for having made him look soft. The truth is that my soldiers and I were lucky no one got seriously hurt, or worse. But on the other hand, there is no way to instill grit and mental fortitude in combatants without putting them at real risk.

That story still comes up every time the team meets up. To this day, none of us can say with any confidence what the right thing to do might have been. Nevertheless, we are all glad to be on the side that dared and succeeded.

After crossing the stream, the team raced south along the dry stream bed of the Hed river. I remember charging across the terrain, surprised by the ease with which I was moving despite the weight of my equipment. They reached HaNegev Junction and found shelter to camouflage themselves in. I came in the morning to inspect them. They had done a pretty good job, I couldn't find most of them. I climbed onto the back of the truck, tossed a mattress on the floor, and went to sleep.

Ten years later, I was called to reserve duty to oversee a similar exercise by another team of cadets. The squad commander had to go on operational duty, so they asked me to fill in for him. I always enjoyed being out in the field, so I readily agreed. During roll call before the exercise, I pointed out to one of the soldiers that his spade was protruding from his pack too much. He didn't bother fixing it. By that time, the army had already updated its protocols, and I was accompanied by an ambulance and a doctor on reserve duty. Years later, that doctor became one of the best neurologists in the country.

The next day, as we were brewing a pot of coffee on a camping stove in the evening, we saw a flare go up. At the same time, a distress signal came in over the radio. I jumped into the jeep, and the doctor jumped into the ambulance; we rushed towards the spot where the flare had been shot from. When we reached the place, we found a soldier lying unconscious with all his equipment on. We stripped him of his gear and the doctor tried to stir him awake, but to no avail. Suddenly, I recalled the roll call. I checked the base of his skull, and found a contusion with slight bleeding. It was the spade. The doctor rushed him to the nearby hospital. We went back, and the exercise carried on. A while later, I learned how the story had ended: when he woke up a couple of days later, he didn't remember anything and didn't recognize anyone, not even his parents. It took two whole weeks before he regained his memory, and went on to become a leading soldier in his team.

By nightfall, the soldiers left their hideouts, packed their gear, and disappeared into the darkness. In the middle of the night, they reunited and teamed up with me at a firing range. Our assignment was to storm a dummy artillery battery. We completed our objective, and retreated with loaded stretchers. The team then dispersed again, everyone heading off by themselves.

I clearly remember going through that exercise when I was a cadet myself. I'd descended the Dimona range, crossed the empty highway, and strode towards the next hill. My legs had hurt I'd felt like my feet were being prodded with a red-hot iron rod. My back had ached from carrying my pack, spasms in my thigh muscles from bearing all that weight while scaling a ridge. Perversely, I'd enjoyed the feeling of overcoming the pain and striding, almost galloping, forward. That feeling of elation had been cut short by dogs menacingly surrounding me every time I passed by a Bedouin campsite. Their incessant hoarse barking had compromised my stealth and silence. One dog in particular had stuck to my heels and simply wouldn't leave me alone, even as I got far from the camp. Without thinking, I'd turned around, loaded my rifle, held it by my waist and released a round. Lucky for both of us, I'd missed. He'd turned on his heels and scampered away.

The following night, I settled in at a windy facility in Rosh Zohar, overlooking Arad. The soldiers' assignment was to sneak in and lay dummy explosives in the facility. Admittedly, I made a poor sentinel and mostly just napped. One of the soldiers audaciously left me a note saying: too bad you're sleeping, we wanted to say hello.

The following night saw them arrive one by one to perform a complex combat exercise, in which they faced a large opposing force. Of course, the opposing force was comprised of cardboard figures, but with the unit's top brass all coming down to examine the drill, it was certainly a challenge. I remember when it had been my turn to perform that exercise— I'd been absolutely inspired that night. I'd performed with even more precision and intensity than I later would in actual combat. I remember my squad commander patting me on the back, saying: good job. For me, that was better than receiving a medal of honor.

Later, the soldiers fell into one line. I led them at a measured pace to the Roman battery, to conquer Masada. We were scaling the steep incline when colored smoke grenades went off all around us, flares and fireworks exploding above us. It's impossible to put that feeling into words. Only one who has dreamed, dared, tried, and succeeded could imagine it.

On top of Masada, in the ruins of Herod's palace, we swore allegiance to the flag and to the country. We fired a full magazine of tracer bullets into the air, and became fully fledged combatants. We put on the unit's insignia for the first and last time— the insignia is secret, and the pins are never worn in public.

CHAPTER 12

SLEEP AND DREAM: MORTAL DANGER

When you are a soldier or an officer on frequent operational duty, your internal world gets deeply intertwined with the outside world, sometimes with harrowing consequences.

I stand amidst a large crowd. People are huddled in pairs and groups against the magnificent backdrop of a brilliantly colorful hall. They talk amongst themselves but I can't hear them. Someone is leading me through the crowd but I can't see who. We reach a secluded corner, and I stand in front of a tall old man with a magnificent white beard.

He looks at me with a penetrating gaze, and without warning says: "You will die on the night between the 27th and 28th of October." The utterance lingers in the space between us. I get sucked out of the scene and wake up in a cold sweat. I'm in my room in the officers' quarters of the base. It's a hot Saturday in the middle of August. I feel disturbed by the dream, but not as disturbed as I am by the fan not working. Besides, it's August. There's plenty of time till October. I fall back asleep.

Finally, an operation. In the morning, we roll into al-Khiam— a village in South Lebanon— in our trucks. The village has been abandoned since Operation Litany. Each team takes a house and settles in. The soldiers review and restock their gear, adding a magazine here, a grenade there, and ammunition belts to their already engorged combat vests. I say nothing; I'll make them take it all out later during roll call. I go to the command briefing and the intelligence briefing, and come back with maps and diagrams. The team huddles around me, and we once again go over the roles we already know so well. We've been waiting a long time for this, a combat operation, a three-pronged raid on three terrorist targets in Ramat Arnoun in Lebanon. We are a senior, experienced, and well-trained team; there's a bit of tension in the air, but no fear. I've commanded this team for over two years now. I know each and every soldier's strengths and weaknesses, and they know me.

American cigarettes are cheap in Lebanon, but we're not allowed to take them out of the country. Military Police check at the gate and confiscate what they find.

Christian-Arab kids run around us hawking cigarettes. Since we'll be going out on a helicopter, all the smokers shove as many packs as they can into their vests. I go out to smoke in the sun. I light a Marlboro cigarette from a soft red pack, and suddenly it dawns on me: today is October 27th! Tonight will be the night between the 27th and 28th of October. I feel my blood curdle. The cigarette turns bland, my chest closes up, and the bright sunny sky seems to cloud over. After a couple of moments, I relax and laugh at myself for being so superstitious. I go back inside to the sound of incessant bickering and joking.

In the evening, trucks take us to the village of 'Ayun. Before loading the trucks, I inspect the soldiers and their gear, more a common reminder than an inspection. I tighten a strap here, loosen one there, and make one of the soldiers take his helmet with him despite his insistence he doesn't need it. I direct the driver all throughout the bumpy ride, until we reach 'Ayun village. We hop off the truck between the houses of the village, our gear already loaded on our backs; we cock our rifles, put a bullet in the barrel, and lock our weapons; the gunner puts a belt in the machine gun's chamber. Under the cover of darkness, we cross the ridge and start the steep descent towards the Litany River. As we make our way down, the lights in the houses of the village suddenly flick on and off. That's quite possibly a signal to alert the enemy of our presence, although the electric grid in South Lebanon is notoriously shoddy and it could be nothing. We walk in a long line, and despite the tension in the air, jokes make their way back across the line. We carefully cross the Litany without trouble. The ascent up Ramat Arnon is long and arduous, and our shoes are wet from crossing the river, but we are all in peak physical shape. We stop for a short drink, every pair sharing a canteen. I share mine with my signaler and feel an odd sense of elation— I'm leading a team of warriors that I trained and instructed, and we're going to confront the enemy.

We head out again and hasten our steps. The incline slowly levels out, meaning we are already on Ramat Arnoun and are nearing our target. We reach the staging point. I lead my team quietly to the right side of the force's three-pronged formation. We lie on the ground 300 feet away from a stone wall, behind which lies the enemy camp.

We lie there motionless. The night is extremely quiet, and we wait for the other forces to take up their positions. We're 300 feet from the enemy, and I fall asleep— even though I'm not particularly tired, and don't tend to usually fall asleep. I sleep for twenty whole minutes, a deep, dreamless sleep. Jacob, my signaler, stirs me awake and whispers: "We're going." I wake up at once, energy pulsing through my body. We advance low to the ground, when all of a sudden the night erupts into a shower of bullets. We leg it over the stone fence, where we are finally in sight of the enemy camp and a cluster of bunkers. "Fire!" I shout, and the team unloads a furious barrage at the complex. Our illuminating grenades run out (a fact that sentenced the person who was supposed to carry them to years of jokes at his expense). I stand up and identify targets, completely disregarding the danger, shooting tracer bullets to mark the boundaries of the sector.

I give the order to storm the complex, and we advance in a line while shooting. Adrenaline is coursing through my veins: I can see sharper, run faster, I'm focused, and every muscle in my body is synched and coordinated. I feel like an indestructible war machine. We reach the bunkers and split into squads. As I run around the bunker, I feel a round of bullets whistle between my legs. I lift up my rifle and see the company commander running towards me and shooting. I shout for him to stop, and he stands in his place. We surround the bunkers. We shoot inside, and they shoot back. We toss a smoke grenade inside and wait. The terrorists scamper out, and we pick them off one by one. One of the soldiers yells to me that some of them got away; I take the gunner with me and we run to the road. Three terrorists are hightailing it down the road. The gunner holds his machine gun to his waist and discharges a long round which hits the running figures and sends them flying like cardboard targets at a range.

We blow up the bunkers and team up with the main force to retreat. It turns out we've taken a hostage, an old Arab man. My team is assigned to lead him back. He is barefoot, and is slowing our progress. The commander of the force orders us to open a stretcher. Two of my soldiers, farm boys from Tel Adashim, take offense to the idea of carrying a hostage: "He'll walk," they promise. And walk he does. In fact, run is a more accurate verb.

We reach the clearance point. Distant rapid thudding sounds suggest the helicopter is nearby. Suddenly it's right above us, a giant Sikorsky helicopter; the sound of its motor is deafening. The helicopter lands like a huge grasshopper, and we rush inside. Rendezvousing with a chopper in the middle of enemy territory is like getting back to the safety of a mother's embrace. I stand by the entrance and count my soldiers. I signal to the flight mechanic that everyone's here and that we can go. He closes the trap, and the helicopter takes off. I stand close to the tail in the back, when all of a sudden I'm swept off my feet. I land straight on my backside in the middle of the chopper. A machine gun round fired from Beaufort Castle penetrated the body of the chopper near the tail; the thrust of the hit tilts the helicopter, and I'm sent flying. If I had remained standing in place, I would have been hit. Luckily, the bullets fizz inside but don't hit anything vital. The pilot steadies the helicopter and flies back south.

We land in a military airfield in Israel. We huddle up, sitting down on our helmets. A faint light appears in the early morning sky. I light a contraband Marlboro cigarette from a soft red pack and burst out laughing in relief. I made it out alive. The dream was just nonsense.

The joking around continues, until a helicopter carrying the Paratrooper reconnaissance company lands. They alight with dark, gloomy faces, carrying a stretcher with a body spread across it. The company commander, whom I knew, was killed. It turns out the Golani reconnaissance company opened fire prematurely. We were safely sneaking up to the fence at that moment, but the Paratroopers were on low ground; the terrorists opened fire before they could reach their positions. Suddenly the whole thing snaps back to reality; it doesn't feel like a game anymore. We look across at each other, and are glad to be alive.

The following night, I'm sleeping on an iron cot in the officer's quarters. Suddenly, the door swings open and the figure of an eyeless soldier blocks the light. I look at him, rooted to the spot: "I am your absolution," he says through a clenched mouth, and vanishes. I wake up soaked in sweat. We gotta fix that damned fan… I grumpily think to myself. I go back to sleep.

CHAPTER 13

WET COOPERATION

In the early 1980s, Erez found himself in a cold and wet operation.

A team of combatants is meant to carry out operations which sometimes require skillsets that fall outside the purview of its expertise. The team then acquires those skills in training.

We were sent to train with Shayetet 13, the navy's elite sea-to-land commando unit, ahead of an upcoming joint operation. Traditionally, there's tension between the two units, which are considered to be the army's finest. They referred to us as Tizonim, a plural noun derived from a slang verb suggesting all we do is run around hills, or Tizkim, a term incorporating the Arabic word for "ass." We called them Uchtabutim, meaning "octopuses," a particularly mean jab considering that was what they called the defensive diver unit; they couldn't stand that we compared them to a unit they considered inferior. Around the time of the joint operation, tension between the units was even higher than usual: a couple of weeks earlier, a shayat – a navy commando, one of their own – was killed while inspecting a sea vessel for our unit. The shayat warned that it was too dangerous to go in the water, but our commander insisted. So he went in, and never came out. They disliked us, and we disliked them. It was an ugly, childish rivalry.

We were assigned sleeping quarters above the navy commando cadet school. Things got off to a bad start, when we were accused of stealing their clothes which they had hung to dry; in retaliation, they refused to allow us to eat in the combatants' mess hall. Later, they took us out to a physical fitness training session, which quickly escalated into a wild contest: it started off with a run, a contest in which we could easily outperform them; so they made sure to take us out to sand dunes which they knew like the back of their hands, and with which we struggled. We refused to let the fact that we were having a hard time show, and gave everything we had to match them. But then they made a mistake: they took us to the rope yard to practice a standard 20-foot rope climb using only our hands. In our unit, rope climbing was a religion. Even the weakest among us could easily climb up and down 5-6 times without a break. We were very pleased when it became evident that the brawny and burly shayatim couldn't even climb half the amount that we could… Our smugness lasted until 6AM the following morning, when they took us out to the bay behind their base for a "clawing" exercise. "Clawing" is a grueling swimming technique in which you propel yourself forward using nothing but fins on your feet. We didn't know the first thing about "clawing," and nothing could have prepared us for such a nightmare. You lie and float on your back, and beat the water with your fin-clad feet. The shayatim sliced through the salty sea water like torpedoes, while we struggled to merely stay afloat.

Over the coming weeks, they taught us everything we needed to know ahead of the operation. They weren't even too smug about it, provoking us no more than one would expect. They taught us how to put on our wetsuits; they envied the new high-quality gear our unit had provided us. They could only dream of having such suits— lighter, thinner, and easier to move in. A wetsuit keeps your body warm in the water, but becomes hot as an oven and heavy as an anchor as soon as you're back on dry land.

They taught us how to seal the barrel of our rifles when we submerged, as well as how to clean and grease it when we came out. Once again, our gear was superior to theirs. They still used Russian AK-47s, assuming (correctly) they would fire in any condition. We were using the Colt AR-14 made mostly from plastic alloys, meaning it didn't rust as easily.

We trained together, trying to synthesize our different approaches to warfare. As far they were concerned, brute force and aggression was the only way to go about it, while we preferred patience and precision. It didn't gel. They couldn't understand why we insisted on repeating the same drill over and over while timing ourselves, let alone why we insisted on doing it in full gear. They put weights in their combat vests, but we insisted on magazines. They didn't understand the point of messing up their gear, while we were adamant that was the only way to see if they could endure the water.

In terms of the chain of command, things did not go any smoother. We insisted on planning everything to the finest detail, while they wanted to leave some room for maneuvering and making calls in the field. When we prepared a dossier of potential situations and complications, they flat-out refused to go over it, claiming we were overdoing it.

We made progress. We no longer swallowed seawater when "clawing," and even the long bay was starting to seem like a manageable distance to swim. They got used to timing their exercises. Their company commander broke his hand, so a squad commander was brought in to replace him. For some reason, the shayatim were significantly bigger and brawnier than us: we didn't know if Shayetet 13 chose only the big ones to start with, whether the cadets grew bigger due to constantly training in the sea, or whether it was just the bigger ones that made it through their qualification course. We, for the most part, were built smaller and lighter. Uzi Dayan once said: "In the unit, what matters are your head and your balls. And the closer they are to each other, the better." The shayatim said that was nothing but pocket-sized excuses for pocket-sized soldiers.

When our water skills reached a satisfactory level, we started practicing for the operation itself. It was nigh on impossible to impress the patience necessary for stealth upon the shayatim's inherently gung-ho approach to warfare. In the end, we had to change our plans and leave them behind to secure the rear.

We went back to the unit for preparations, and the unit commander called me in to ask how it went. I explained the gulf between our worldviews, and offered my analysis as to why that was. He informed me that he was assigning a veteran squad commander named Golan to the operation, both because the shayatim would never accept me as their commander, and also to look out for me. I didn't like the idea, but there was little I could do about it.

We continued to practice. Senior officers came to observe and offered irritating comments. We made tweaks and adjustments, and carried on practicing. The shayatim vehemently argued that we were overdoing the preparations, and that they would have already carried out the operation a long time ago if it was up to them. We answered that it was precisely for that reason that every operation of theirs ends up facing enemy fire. They said that was the way they liked it, that unlike us they liked fighting.

Tuesday was the day the shayatim would come down to the Tavern pub. We started going on Tuesdays as well. The beer flowed like water, and lighthearted banter often escalated into out-and-out brawls. But at the same time, we struck up some genuine friendships which eased the burden we imposed on them with our endless preparations.

I quickly became persona non-grata among the navy commando command chain. They detested my endless jabs about their impatience. I became very grateful to have Golan backing me up.

Finally, the day of the operation arrived. We drove out to the docks and loaded our gear onto a ship. Unlike us, the shayatim sailed out with their ship anchored two nautical miles (2.3 miles) off their coastal base. Admittedly, their entrance was much more impressive.

The following day, we sailed out. The ship was packed to the brim, without so much as a place to sit. The crowded deck prompted us to take over the skipper's cabin. A mix of our guys and shayatim crowded in the small cabin. Someone found the skipper's bar, but after some deliberation, we chose to leave it be. Tempting as it was, we did have an operation to perform…

At last light, the rubber boats were lowered into the water on the side further from the shore, even though we had sailed far out into the sea anyway. We loaded our gear, which by then had become very familiar, and made our way onto the wobbly boats. I remember I didn't feel scared. It all seemed very surreal and detached.

The rubber boats sped away, and we had to hold on tight to avoid falling off. We were sprayed with droplets of cold, salty seawater. Despite being covered in gear from head to toe, we were starting to feel cold. Finally, we got sufficiently close to the shoreline. The boat operators killed the engines and let inertia carry the boats forward. We formed a long, straight line of softly gliding boats— a testament to the operators' impressive skills. As the night sky grew darker, so too did the air grow colder. The small expeditionary force silently took to the water.

I went into the sea, my chest immediately seizing up from the shock of the freezing water. I started making small motions with my feet to get my fins going and stabilize myself. We began "clawing" in formation, with the navy squad commander leading the way. We turned around and looked at the beach. We didn't need night vision equipment to see that there were people there.

We waited. As we lingered in the water, I felt I was starting to drown. Despite insisting on practicing in full gear, the actual accumulated weight we carried was far greater than what we'd trained in. The small movements with my feet did little to help. My head occasionally submerged, and I was starting to feel panicked. Suddenly I felt a large hand grab hold of me: the navy squad commander put his mouth by my inflatable flotation belt, and blew with the ferocity that only a shayat could muster. I instantly felt my buoyancy double.

The beach refused to clear of people, and we had to carry on waiting. The cold was becoming a problem, and the soldiers on the boats were losing their patience. We remained in this condition for over an hour. We were freezing, our hands gone completely numb.

And then it happened. A small fishing boat with a dinky little motor set out of the harbor. Unbeknownst to him, he was heading straight towards our rubber boats. We looked on helplessly. It was down to the commander of the rubber boat fleet to call this play.

The soldiers in the boats could have scattered, could

have taken out the fisherman, could have apprehended him… but instead, they did nothing. The small fishing boat sailed breezily between the row of rubber boats like a general inspecting roll call. After passing our boats, the fisherman turned his vessel around and passed through them again—as if refusing to believe what his eyes just saw. He carried on unmolested and made his way back to the harbor.

A ruckus started. No one knew what to do. We didn't know if we'd been. To solve our dilemma, a Soviet-made Syrian battleship left the harbor towards us, and a hasty retreat promptly followed. As the boats retreated, no one thought to come pick us up.

We found ourselves alone, nine soldiers abandoned a couple of hundred feet away from the Syrian coastline. We started laughing out of fear and tension. We slowly started "clawing" away from the beach. After putting a safe distance between us and the shore, we activated a radio to signal our location: if someone wanted to come looking for us, now they had a way to find us.

The cold was getting worse: our body temperatures dropped, and none of us could feel our hands and feet. We tried keeping ourselves warm by "clawing," by urinating in our wetsuits, and by sticking close together. Our lightweight wetsuits turned out to be inefficient, and hardly retained our body heat. The shayatim put us in the middle of the huddle to heat us up, which did help a little.

Just before dawn, we heard the rattle of a helicopter engine. The sound was music to our ears, but we were worried they wouldn't be able to spot us. We all turned on our xenon flashlights, which we carried for this scenario exactly. The helicopter reached us, stabilized itself above our heads, and lowered a cable. The shayatim showed us how to bolt ourselves to the cable, and the helicopter pulled us up one by one.

The flight mechanic gave us his earphones. Since we wore no rank insignias, he didn't know who commanded the force and handed the earphones to a random soldier. The soldier, a shayat, uncharacteristically handed the earphones over to me—as if to say: you got us into this mess, now you get us out!

The pilots were as cold and calculated as ever. They told me they had to take us in two rounds, since there were too many of us. I explained to the pilot that the soldiers in the water were in critical condition, and asked where he was taking us. He replied that he was flying over to a nearby warship with a landing pad, about 20 minutes in each direction. I asked where our boat was, and the pilots told me it was about 5 minutes' flight away. We agreed they'd drop us off in the water by the boat. On the way, I was informed there was some sort of showdown going on, with no shots yet fired. It turned the Syrian battleship and our ship were maneuvering in range of each other's radar. They had powerful radars. The Israeli navy sent out two warships to help us. A warship is an incredible machine, so the enemy's inferior ships didn't dare so much as go near them. But either way, we had to rush over to our ship that was waiting for us—it had to get out of Syrian territory as soon as possible.

We reached the ships, and had to lower ourselves into the water. We had no idea what to do, and the shayatim had to demonstrate for us. The conclusion was unavoidable: we did not cover enough possible scenarios in preparation for the operation. It was simply not possible to acquire so much professional proficiency in such a short time. The flight mechanic held me up as the helicopter got as close to the water as it could, and dropped me down. I jumped legs first, like the shayatim told us. I sank like a stone, the water was freezing, and my flotation belt floated me back up. I "clawed" towards the back of the ship, and was quickly pulled out of the water. Finally—solid ground! Albeit made of iron, but anything was better than that black watery abyss.

Aboard the ship, it was chaos. The sailors yelled at us to get out of their way. There wasn't an inch of space, but everyone desperately looked for a place to sit down and rest. I elbowed my way to the skipper's cabin, took off my gear, changed into a dry uniform, and slumped in the corner.

The cabin was desperately overcrowded. Everyone was tired, and an oppressive feeling of failure lingered in the air. Someone rediscovered the skipper's bar, and this time there was nothing to hold us back. There were expensive whiskeys there which we sipped straight from the bottle as if they were canteens of tap water. None of us had even tasted expensive whiskey before. A nice warm feeling pervaded our bodies. We were tired and hungry, and became intoxicated almost immediately. Pretty soon, the place was a mess of drunken rambling, bickering, and brawling. It was intolerable, but we didn't have the energy to get up and get out of there.

After two brawling drunks toppled over me, I finally made the effort and got out of the cabin. Dawn had broken, and the ship sailed south on the open sea. I lit a cigarette after going a whole night without nicotine. I felt dizzy. We knew we'd failed, and that we'd be haunted by this failure. It was already clear to me then that our ceaseless insistence on avoiding contact had inhibited the shayatim and caused them to stand by passively when the small fishing boat passed us. I wondered how long it would take for us to get blamed for that.

We arrived off the shore of the navy base in the

afternoon. The shayatim took about an hour to unload their equipment into boats, and then sailed off to their base. We continued on to Haifa Port, our ship now half empty. We unloaded our equipment onto trucks sent especially from the unit. We drove back, and spent an hour silently unloading the trucks.

After that, I finally went to take a long, hot shower. I must have spent at least an hour in the shower, before crashing down on my bed. Just as I was about to sink into the sweetest of deep slumbers, I felt someone violently shaking my shoulder and calling my name repeatedly. My consciousness slowly resurfaced, I opened my eyes and focused on the sight of a soldier with a scared look in his eyes. When he saw that I was up, he almost yelled: "We can't find Assi! No one can remember the last time they saw him!"

I jumped out of bed and ran to the telephone in the hall. I then decided I couldn't manage this situation from a hallway, so I put on a pair of shorts and ran as fast as I could down to the radio room. I pounded on the door until a soldier who was sleeping there groggily woke up.

"Just a minute," she called out.

"I don't have a minute, open up NOW!" I yelled.

I leaped inside when the door opened. To my surprise, it was Tal, Eitan's ex-girlfriend. She was only half dressed, causing us both to feel embarrassed.

"You look great like that…" I said. "Now get me the unit commander, the operations officer, and the operations branch officer."

She didn't lose her cool, going over to make the call while laughing, clearly enjoying the compliment.

"If I'd have known you were going to storm in like that, I would have waited for you naked…" she said.

"Be careful what you wish for," I replied. "Did you get hold of him already?"

I brought the unit commander and the rest of them up to speed. They immediately alerted the commander of the navy, the air force search-and-rescue units, and just about the entire army. Meanwhile, I found myself gawking at Tal's long bare legs. She acted like she didn't notice.

"Couldn't he possibly have just fallen asleep on the boat?" she asked.

"What was that?" I asked, snapping back to reality after staring at her spellbinding legs.

"Couldn't he simply be on the boat?" she repeated impatiently, slightly pulling up her oversized long-sleeved T-shirt, teasingly revealing the magnificent curve where her upper hip met her bottom.

"You know what, maybe…" I said, unable to look away. "Let's give them a call."

After several failed attempts, she managed to get hold of the base in Haifa and the officer in charge of the ship. He answered in a sleepy voice. I asked him if I may have forgotten a soldier onboard.

"There's a soldier pacing around here, looking for a ride out of the base," he answered.

"Can you please call him over to the phone?" I asked, praying silently that it was Assi.

A couple of moments later, Tal extended one of her long legs and pressed it up against mine, making my blood boil. I reached over and placed my hand on her hip. She didn't pull back, so I left it there.

It turns out it really was Assi! After a night of drinking, he'd simply fallen asleep in a dark corner. Nothing had stirred him—neither the stops nor the unloading. I told him to wait there, and that I'd send a car out to get him. I let everyone know, including the motor pool officer. I let out a sigh of relief, and crashed down on the small cot Tal had been sleeping in before I rudely burst into the radio room.

"That was a close one…" I said. "I was sure I was going to have to go back out to the sea, or to Syria."

Tal gave me a look I wasn't sure how to read.

"Well, I'm gonna go. I have to go to sleep," I said, but didn't move.

"You're not going anywhere, mister," she said. She got

up, locked the door, turned off the lights, and took off her shirt.

"I thought you'd never do that," I quietly uttered. Those were the last words I would say for the next hour or so.

During the briefing the following morning, the commander of the navy said: "The operation was a success, but the patient is dead."

"What's that supposed to mean?" the commander-in-chief of the army said. He wasn't the type to be easily dismissed with vague metaphors.

"It means what it means…" the commander of the navy replied.

"For your sake and everyone involved, that better not mean what I think that means," the commander-in-chief said sternly.

What was the end of that exchange? I don't know. We were marked as a team that had failed, meaning we went into deep freeze. Essentially, we had become "non-operational"— not officially, but very much so for all practical matters. Time trudged along slowly after that, long and dull, but on the other hand it gave me the time to develop an interesting relationship with Tal— a relationship marred with feelings of guilt for having an affair with the ex-girlfriend of a soldier of mine.

CHAPTER 14

WALKING OPERATION

In those days, there were several ways to mobilize an operation: by vehicle, by aircraft, or on foot. There were interesting combinations as well. But the most distinguished and revered of all were always walking operations, carried out with nothing but your own two feet, your back, and an unflagging will.

Finally, another operation. After the debacle with the navy commandos, we were frozen out for several months. The incident had happened in open water and we were at fault for the operation's failure—and a team that has failed, for whatever reason, is always marked. We could read the faces of senior officers, looking at us and thinking: You had your chance. Other teams teased us as well: we were pegged as the team that went "from unbridled to idle."

To stay sharp, I subjected my team to a rigorous daily

fitness regime: we would first run a couple of miles, and then take a few rounds scaling up and down the rope; we would do chin-ups, hand "walking" over parallel bars, and concluded this part with push-ups on the parallel bars. We repeated this routine five times. After that, we'd either do hundreds of sit-ups, or instead drive down to Sidna 'Ali beach, where we would sprint up the road's gruelingly steep incline; we would then sprint back down, go into the water and run a hundred paces, followed by push-ups and sit-ups. We'd repeat that routine ten times. Occasionally, we ran gladiator rounds— or "Juantorena" rounds (named after the legendary Cuban Olympic runner, Alberto Juantorena, who was at the peak of his popularity back then) as the soldiers called it: we would run in a row, and the last runner would spring up to the head of the row; the soldier now last would spring up to the head of the row, and so we'd repeat for 6 miles. Our muscles grew and our backs strengthened. But we were losing patience.

My only solace was that Tal turned out to be a passionate and creative lover. We thoroughly enjoyed our time together.

I hounded the office secretaries to remind the unit commander of my existence. I intentionally sat down next to him in the mess hall. I sucked up to the intelligence officer and his deputy, so they'd bring my name up in discussions of operations. I even tried to sweet-talk a company commander I detested—all to no avail. Every evening, we'd play bridge in the new rec hall. We'd go out for drinks at the Tavern, where we often came across shayatim whom we still blamed for botching that operation. On several occasions, confrontations escalated to brawls. As previously mentioned, we would call them uchtabutim (octopuses) and they called us tizonim (hill-runners); for highly-trained, testosterone-charged, aggressive young men, those nicknames were enough to spark violent scuffles.

My frustration mounted, so when the unit commander finally called me into his office, I was about to give him a serious piece of my mind. It took me a good couple of minutes to realize what he was saying: "Walking operation." I looked at him incredulously. The unit hadn't carried out a proper walking operation in years.

"But it's still on the fence," he quickly warned, seeing my excitement. "If you don't prove that your team is able to keep the schedule to a T, I won't send the operation for approval."

I wanted to hug him, but just barely managed to restrain myself. I walked out of the office with a stupid smile plastered on my face. The secretaries, who already knew, congratulated me. I assembled the team and broke the news.

"This is a test," I told them, "we've been given a second chance after messing up the first one. You're going to work hard— I'll see to that— and you'll rise to every challenge."

I went in for a meeting with the operations officer working on this project. We prepared a training program, recalled a discharged soldier into active service to oversee the team's professional training, worked out a program for walking practices, and then for simulation models. All in all— it took three months of preparation.

The sports officer detailed the fitness program he had worked out for the team. I looked at it and burst out laughing. "You must be joking," I told him, "this is chump change. You're more than welcome to come see the actual workouts my team will be doing. Do you know where the tires and weighted vests are stored?" I asked him.

"I can look…" he replied.

"You'd better find them," I concluded.

The soldiers came to their first fitness session wearing shorts and running shoes. I could see the apprehension in their eyes— they knew me well, and were afraid with good reason. We did the usual round of running and rope climbing, but then I took them to the 400-meter dash dirt track. There they found car tires with ropes tied to them, the other end waiting to be tied around their waists.

"Five rounds," I yelled, "and give it everything you've got! Two-minute breaks between each round." The first batch of soldiers tied the ropes to their waists, myself included. The first round was hard— our legs swelled and our backs hurt. Our lungs burned from the effort, and our pulses skyrocketed. I wasn't sure I could even finish the second round. Half the team vomited in the third round, but got right back to it. The fourth and fifth rounds were out of this world. We were beyond exhaustion in the end. "We add another round every session," I informed the anguished soldiers.

I took them to the rope yard, where 40-pound weighted vests were waiting for them. We went on a 400-yard run, followed by a 25-foot rope climb using only our hands, then "walking" forward on the parallel bars using our arms. We repeated the routine five times.

"Are we going to do this every day as well?" Adi asked in exasperation.

"Of course," I answered sternly. "You'll be beasts by the end of this program."

"Or cripples…" someone remarked.

"If anyone wants to quit, you're more than welcome to do so," I said. No one budged.

We had a surprise waiting for us in the mess hall: a separate table was set up for us, where we were served high-carb meals tailored for us by the unit doctor. The whole unit was watching us. We ate like starved pigs.

The doctor was supposed to come with us on the operation, but he didn't show up for fitness training on Monday. I went to see him in the infirmary. To my astonishment, I found him with Tal in a position that left little to the imagination. After our initial shock, she scampered away and I told him: "You need to come to practice, or I'm not taking you with me."

"I'm over 30 years old, my body still hasn't recovered from yesterday's practice…" he answered frankly.

"Doctor," I told him, "I could care less. You either show up, or you're out. Come down and do what you can," I demanded.

He did start coming, but inconsistently. We would pay dearly for that, later.

I stopped seeing Tal, not just because of the incident with the doctor, but mainly because I simply didn't have the time. But since I never said anything to her about it, she interpreted it differently. Either way, I didn't bother worrying over it.

We would wake up early every day, do a light training session, and get breakfast. Until noon, every soldier on the team was busy with professional training pertaining to the operation. After lunch, we'd have our killer training session. We'd spend the evenings after dinner studying maps of the operation's terrain.

I was given an office in the building housing the unit's intelligence department, and was assigned a non-commissioned officer to prepare an intelligence report for me. I sat there for a couple of hours, enjoying having my own office. I carried on with the rest of the preparations from my room in the officers' quarters—that day was the first and last time I bothered going to that dinky little office.

We practiced on Saturdays as well. I limited tire-pulling practice that day to ten rounds, since we had two walking exercises that week. The first exercise was pretty easy— we walked for 25 miles at a pace of about 5 miles per hour without almost any weight on us, just our combat vests and weapons. We took a drinking break every hour. The soldiers breezed through the exercise. The second exercise was an uphill track. It was significantly harder, and our bodies were still aching from our daily training. Nevertheless, we kept the times we'd designated for ourselves to finish the exercises.

The third week was tough. We went on with the daily fitness regime, and completed two weighted walking exercises across a steep, hilly course. That weekend, the doctor dropped a bombshell on me: two of the soldiers were suffering from hernia fractures and were unable to carry on training, meaning they were ruled out of the operation. This was especially disastrous because one of them was Jacob, my trusted signaler. But the problem was bigger than that: we only had one spare soldier training with us for this exact purpose, to step in for an incapacitated team member.

On my way back, Tal pulled me over to talk.

"Erez, you're avoiding me," she protested.

"I'm not, I'm just really busy."

"Listen, I can explain…" she went on.

"You don't owe me an explanation. You never promised me anything, nor I you."

"Still, you're avoiding me," she insisted.

"I've already told you, I'm busy. You know that."

"It's an excuse, Erez."

"Maybe. But it's a good one," I said, and went back to my room.

As I sat there, worrying about the shape of my team, Regev—the soldier with exceptional driving skills—came to see me. He had been removed from my team and assigned to the operational drivers division about a year ago. He came to ask to rejoin the team.

"You haven't walked for a year," I replied dismissively, "and besides, you're already three weeks behind in training."

"I can handle it," he decisively asserted.

He was tall and strong, a wild and uncouth boy. He

was hard to rein in, but his grit and determination were second to none. Finally, I agreed, and didn't regret that decision for even a second. When the moment of truth came, he was as fierce as a lion.

In operations such as this, the squad commander is usually assigned an older squad commander as his deputy, to draw on his experience and help make decisions in the field. In our case, that was impossible because no one could walk this operation's axis without proper preparations first. Eventually, I was assigned a younger deputy. He was also wild— a perfect fit for me and my team.

It was time to prove we were truly up to the task. After two months of rigorous training, our backs no longer hurt. My soldiers and I could now go through twelve rounds of tire-pulls and twelve rounds of weighted runs, and be ready for more. The intelligence department planned a simulation axis of advance for us. I went over it with a stereoscope (a depth-simulating device), a map, and aerial photos. It looked fine.

We assigned positions within the force and planned the distribution of weights. It came out to a substantial 120-130 pounds per soldier. I briefed the team, and we rode out to our departure point. We left the trucks at last light. I conducted one last roll call, and patted each of them on the back. Before heading out, I quietly said:

"This is it, my friends, this is what we've been training so hard for. If we prove we can do this tonight, we'll get the green light for an operation we'll remember for the rest of our lives."

We started walking quietly under the cover of darkness. We reacted to dangers we encountered in the field: we stopped, froze, and advanced. I issued a command using a designated whistle, pssssst, which sent the artificial tooth I had flying out of my mouth. I hesitated for a second, but quickly realized there was nothing I could do about it. From that moment on, I carried out the operation missing one of my front teeth.

We dashed across the terrain like antelopes. I walked at the front of the force carrying light gear, while the rest of the team lugged the weight behind me in anguished silence. When the terrain was flat, I walked at a fast pace and the soldiers had to run to keep up. At inclines, I walked at a fast, steady pace, and the poor soldiers suffered: when carrying heavy weights uphill, you have to lean forward, otherwise the center of gravity shifts back and you topple over. Leaning forward applies tremendous pressure on the lower back, abdominals, and thigh muscles. Add to that dozens of pounds of unevenly distributed weight, and the whole ordeal becomes a veritable nightmare. A couple of minutes are enough to break even a fit and determined individual; we climbed for hours. Every hour, I called a five-minute water break. The soldiers dropped to the ground and wiggled around to reach their canteens, which they gulped down in silent rage. Rage was essential: you couldn't get through such an experience without channeling anger. They hated me, hated the army, hated the unit— and they carried on walking. At the end of the water break, they couldn't get up on their own. I pulled the first one up, and he pulled up the rest. Occasionally, someone would trip; he'd be helped up by the nearest soldier, and we'd move on. After an hour, it seemed impossible to carry on; I had to extend the water breaks, because some of them couldn't get up at all. Five extra minutes later, they were helped up and limped their way onward. Three hours later, we reached a particularly mean incline. I stopped before we started the ascent, which was so steep we had to use all four limbs to climb up. I looked back at the row of human houses trudging along heavily behind me: not a single one of them showed any sign of breaking as they silently awaited my command. I knew we were going to make it.

"Break at the top," I said quietly, momentarily breaking operational silence. They looked at me, each hating me in their own way. I smiled at them in the darkness, my front tooth missing, and started climbing. They were close on my tail. No one stopped, no one lagged behind. When we reached the top, we rested. I was kind, and gave them a ten-minute break. We practically ran the final couple of miles. We made excellent time and kept to the schedule. At the end of the track the unit commander was waiting for me, along with a few other senior officers. He shook my hand and said: "Well done." I realized he hadn't trusted that we would make it, which led me to believe there was something behind his decision to assign this operation to my team. If we failed, he could always dismiss us as a poor team. That made me feel a bit better for having cut the axis a mile short without the knowledge of anyone but the intelligence officer.

It wasn't our intention to lie. When we finished planning the axis, we realized we were about two miles short of the actual axis of the operation. Seeing how everything was so neatly coordinated, and not wanting to spoil a good plan, we decided that we would just run one mile back at the end of the track. As it turns out, we made it to the end by the skin of our teeth, so we decided to forget about the extra mile. Either way, we proved we were up to the task: we got the green light.

We went back to training.

One day, about halfway through the training period, the unit commander and I drove down to a meeting at Special Operations headquarters. We sat around the table, four lieutenant colonels, a colonel, and me— a first lieutenant. Right before going into the meeting, I noticed a girl, as pretty as an angel, carrying out some menial chores outside the building. I wanted to go out and talk to her. The big brass was hashing it out, but I drifted away at some point. They were comparing options and weighing risks. I was annoyed they were talking over my head, even though it was my operation. Their voices faded into a monotonous drone in my head, and I was caught off-guard when they suddenly asked my opinion on a matter.

"It's all talk, anyway," I brazenly said, "at the end of the day, it's going to be me out there calling the shots as I see fit."

A stunned silence pervaded the room. I was surprised myself by what I had said, so I got up and left the room. The girl from before wasn't there any longer. I asked where she had gone, and went looking for her. Half an hour later, the unit commander came to look for me. We drove back to the unit together.

"You're an idiot," he said. "I just spent the last hour trying to convince them not to remove you from the operation…"

"Where are they going to find another idiot who can walk that track?" I said boldly.

To his credit, the unit commander was amused by my

insolence and burst out laughing, so I laughed as well.

The following week, the doctor summoned me to his office. There was a package of pills on his table.

"Do you know what these are?" he asked.

"Not a clue."

"These are Benzedrine pills, a powerful stimulant. These'll give you four hours of energy."

"And what happens after four hours?" I asked.

"There's a drop," he admitted.

"What am I supposed to do with these?" I asked, even though I had a pretty clear idea of where he was going with this.

"We need to try this out on the soldiers, so we can use them if the need arises," he said.

I didn't say anything for a couple of moments, so he continued: "You understand this isn't my idea, right?"

I did. I just didn't understand why this hadn't come up before.

"And you know," he went on, "there's nothing serious between me and Tal."

"I don't care if there is. She's a free woman, she can do whatever she wants."

"She asked me to tell you," the doctor said.

"Good. Mission accomplished, then," I sarcastically confirmed.

We tried the pills out on the soldiers. It worked like a charm: a powerful energy boost and a feeling of elation. The drop wasn't so bad either. I earmarked it as an option.

The date of the operation was drawing nearer. We went into battle procedure, meaning from that point on we could be called into action at a moment's notice. Near the end of the battle procedure period, we assembled for a briefing in the presence of the army's Chief of Staff. After a couple officers spoke, I took the stage as planned to present a detailed briefing.

The Chief of Staff and I had had an embarrassing encounter a couple of months back. I'd presented the details of an operation in his presence, and every time I made a grammatical error, he jumped in and corrected me. I started double-thinking before speaking, but still repeated some mistakes, and he got angry. I'd finished that presentation weary and humiliated. He made me nervous, but didn't interrupt this time, even when I kept making mistakes. Near the end of the briefing, he asked me in his typically figurative way: "Say an Arab farmer decides to hump his sheep and spots you, what do you do?"

"I apprehend him and radio in for instructions."

"There is no radio," he challenged me.

"Then I kill him and take the body back with me," I replied.

"And if it's a woman?"

"I kill her and take the body back," I said with feigned confidence.

"A kid?" he insisted.

"Same," I replied.

The Chief of Staff eyeballed me for a minute, and then said: "You're not a kibbutznik, are you?"

"No," I said to the sounds of muffled giggles from the crowd. "I'm from Ashkelon." Muffled giggles erupted into roaring laughter.

The Chief of Staff stressed that we couldn't kill anyone, and that we had to carry the operation out now because we would be signing a peace treaty with Jordan real soon.

We set a date, and the countdown began. Marathon meetings, packing, unpacking, repacking, last-minute upgrades to equipment, selecting the right pair of uniforms (everyone had their own favorite pair best suited to strenuous exertions), greasing boots—long-since rid of any Israeli identification marks— coffee, and endless packs of cigarettes. One more dry run, and light fitness sessions to keep in shape without overexerting ourselves.

And then the day finally came. We went to the mess hall for lunch, and found our separate table packed with everything you could possibly imagine. The entire unit was looking at us. Everyone knew about the operation, to some extent or other. We felt like gladiators about to enter the ring. The operations officer came to our table and informed us that the Prime Minister had sent a telegram: "Best of luck. We won't leave you behind." Someone left a flower on our table, sparking a slew of speculation as to who it was for. At that moment, we were larger than life, Titans descending from above to grace the earth with their presence.

The gear was loaded up and sent ahead. We gathered by the unit headquarters with nothing but our rifles slung over our shoulders. A Sikorsky helicopter approached the base and landed just outside. We strode over with an air of casual arrogance. We didn't put on helmets, and the flight mechanic protested; I dismissed him with a flick of my wrist, and he dropped the matter. The helicopter took off. I looked out of the window and saw the unit getting smaller and smaller.

We had another meal at the gathering point, and loaded our gear on our backs. Final roll call. I inspected each soldier individually, to make sure their gear adhered to operational standards. I made eye contact with each and every one. It was clear we were about to give it our all. I lingered for a minute by the doctor. It was obvious to me he wasn't nearly as prepared as we were, but he was confident.

I lit one last cigarette with my equipment on my back. The sun was setting. We drove off to the departure point, fell into formation, and hurried across the makeshift bridge erected for us by the younger teams. Pats on the backs, a few good lucks muttered under our breath, and we were off.

Right after the bridge, we encountered a thicket. I had spent dozens of hours going over every inch of our axis of advance: I consulted maps and aerial photos, analyzed angles, terrains, and lines of vision. I knew every stone along the axis. But as it turned out, I hadn't studied the thicket by the Jordan River. 300 yards of a clear trail—sounds simple enough. But there was no trail. I went left, then went right, looking for that damned trail, but it was nowhere to be found. I later found out that we had been dropped off a few dozen yards downstream from where we'd planned to land, because crossing the river was easier at that point. But not knowing that at the time, I did what you're supposed to do in such a situation— I went back to the last place I'd identified for certain, and looked for marks indicating a road. There were none. The soldiers were growing testy watching at me walking around in circles. Ami, who had replaced Jacob as my signaler, whispered in my ear: "Let's just cut through the thicket." His words helped snap me out of the anxiety which had momentarily gripped me. I took a deep breath, and led the force right into the thicket. Three minutes later, we were out. I didn't have time to wallow in guilt. I looked back, and started walking. Fast.

The unit commander and the Chief of Staff were both in the command post, together with other senior officers. The secretary who kept the minutes of the operation was Tal. To ease the tension, the unit commander turned to the Chief of Staff and said:

"You know, after this, he should be promoted to captain." Him being me.

"Maybe. Or demoted to private," the Chief of Staff snarled, worried about the time we had already lost.

I was walking fast. I noticed that I'd started sweating a bit too early. I recalled that before the briefing, the intelligence officer had informed me it would be a particularly hot night tonight. I hadn't made much of it at the time, but I now realized that it could be a problem. Increased sweat requires extra hydration, and we hadn't changed the amount of water we'd taken with us.

We left the vicinity of the river, passing close to a lookout point for the Jordanian army. The line of vision was interrupted, so I wasn't worried about being spotted. We hurried down the wide river valley, and climbed the opposing ridge, beyond which were wide open plains.

After a couple of miles in the fields, we encountered

a problem. To our right, 20-30 yards away, were some people sitting around a campfire. Nothing to worry about, but I wanted to steer clear of them. There were greenhouses ahead of us, with open fields in the space between. There was a solitary shack with an open door standing in the field; the light was on, and there was a man inside. Our lookouts had always reported the shack was unmanned, probably because it was facing the other way.

I deliberated on what to do. I couldn't flank the shack to the right, and going left would lengthen our track and force us to cross an open field. My deputy noticed my hesitation, and said: "Let's just cross."

I got my senses together, and gave the order to cross one by one. We made it safely across. We were close enough to see the whites of the eyes of the man in the shack, but he never raised his head. We kept going at a fast pace before our first water break. I could see the doctor was breathing heavily. I approached him, and he signaled to me that he was fine.

We charged on ahead. I changed our formation— a light and agile point team walking several yards ahead of the bulky, heavier remaining soldiers. I walked first, alert to the whole terrain around us, acutely attuned to sniff out the slightest hint of danger; the rest were too weighed down to look around. I had Amir walking to my right wearing head-mounted night-vision goggles. Night-vision goggles significantly increase your vision, but I hated wearing them— I felt restricted by their narrow scope, and felt that they dulled my other senses. I preferred to listen, to smell, and to feel "like a Native American tracker," I always used to say.

We neared the Dead Sea Highway, running north-south through the Jordan Valley. I positioned a lookout to watch both sides. After they reported back that the sector was "clean," we passed through a large culvert under the road. As we walked, we heard footsteps on the road above us. We stopped. It seemed like one of the Jordanian lookouts had called it a night earlier than usual. We waited for them to put some distance between themselves and the road, and continued crossing.

We were over an hour behind schedule, and still hadn't begun to climb. Half an hour's walk later, we reached the rear side of a military camp. We walked along a goat trail which snaked around the fence at a distance of 50-100 yards. Suddenly I saw a light. I froze in my tracks, and the force took a knee where they were.

A sentinel was standing at the gate right in front of us. He couldn't see us from where he was standing, but his position oversaw the path we needed to take. As I watched the Jordanian soldier manning the gate, Ami whispered to me: "Let's go, what could he possibly do?"

I considered it for a moment, acutely aware that we were desperately behind schedule. I called Amir over, who carried a muffled rifle; I pointed at the soldier, and he understood. I clicked my tongue, the force rose back to their feet, and we started walking. I had no doubt that he noticed us, but we'll never know what he made of what he saw. Anyway, that's what I was banking on: he did nothing, and we moved on.

We climbed as fast as we could. We were dripping sweat from head to toe. I skipped one break to try to make up for lost time. The soldiers panted, gasped, and pushed with every drop of energy left in their bodies. Muscles contracted and swelled in our legs, back, and thighs. We felt our bodies were going to burst like balloons. But we carried on anyway.

After two more hours, we reached our destination. We'd cut our delay down to forty minutes. The operation itself went as smoothly as a hot knife through butter. We infiltrated, we obtained, we vanished. We did it so fast that we managed to save another thirty minutes. Our moods were high. We smiled and patted ourselves on the backs.

Now all that was left was to get my team out before dawn. We fell into formation and started walking. Less than an hour later, dehydration started to kick in. When walking at night, you count off every ten minutes: the last soldier in line taps the shoulder of the person in front of him and says one, and that soldier in turn taps the shoulder of the person in front of him and says two, all the way down to the commander. This procedure serves two purposes: first, it maintains a tight walking formation, and secondly, it feeds the commander constant information about his team and formation. When the count was interrupted, I knew we had a problem.

I halted the force. As I suspected, there were large gaps between the soldiers. Soldiers were vomiting with exhaustion. I huddled them together and made sure everyone was drinking. I went up to the doctor; he was spent. He panted heavily, and could barely understand what I was saying to him.

I took the package of Benzedrine and handed each soldier a pill, making sure they swallowed it with ample water. We were still in the mountains, over 12 miles away from the border. I was worried I might have made the call too soon. It would go down to the wire, I feared. I stretched the break for a few more precious moments, and then said quietly but loud enough for everyone to hear: "Listen up. We need to get out of here. Everybody, gather whatever strength you have left. Help each other. I'll walk at a pace that will get us out of here, but you have to stick to me. We're moving in one minute."

They got up groggily, leaning on each other. I started walking slowly, letting them regain their balance. It was hard to pick up the pace because we were walking downhill and could easily tumble down. Walking downhill, your abdominal muscles are put to work stabilizing and keeping your body at an appropriate angle. Walking fast unsettles your balance, and your core muscles are called in to stabilize your center of gravity. The thousands upon thousands of sit-ups we'd drilled in practice were paying off now. We descended with the precision of mountain goats. The Benzedrine kicked in, and we picked up a frightening pace.

I reported to command post, and they suggested we stay back and hide out for the following day. I had to make a decision before we reached the Dead Sea Highway, it would be too crowded from that point on. The unusually hot night left us seriously dehydrated; we drank more than we intended to. We had a 25% reserve, but we were going through it rapidly. What ultimately tipped the scale against staying was the physical state of some of the soldiers. I was worried another day in the field would put them at serious risk.

We moved on. We passed by the military camp at a near-running pace; the sentinel didn't even wake up. We reached the Dead Sea Highway and crossed it without even stopping for a lookout; it was 3 AM, and I simply assumed it would probably be vacant.

To avoid a repeat of what had happened near the thicket when we first crossed, I chose to follow an alternative route back. The only problem was that we had learned its axis the other way around. To navigate the route, my point man had to feed me the compass angles (azimuth) after having reversed them. But he was exhausted, and made a mistake on a couple of occasions. "Just give me the angles," I whispered to him acridly, "I'll reverse them myself." To compound the incredible pressure I was under, I now had to worry about adding or subtracting 180° to every angle the rest of the way back.

Dehydration clashed with the pills... The rapid expenditure of energy resulted in accelerated dehydration. Some soldiers vomited again. My deputy took the doctor's pack, and soldiers helped each other wherever they could. Our progress slowed. I had to stop and let soldiers close the gaps opening up between them. About a half an hour later, we stopped for a water break. The soldiers were lying on the ground, barely holding onto consciousness. I huddled them together.

"We have about 6 miles to go and a little over an hour to get there," I said. "This is the last break from here to the river. I'm going to run forward, and you stick to me like leeches. Finish all your water. If you want another pill, tell me. Get ready, we leave in five minutes."

The soldiers drank, and helped those who struggled to drink on their own. I forced some of them to take another Benzedrine pill. We got up and tightened the straps of our backpacks. I looked at my team and chuckled. A wolf's chuckle.

"Come on, you animals! Let's do this!" I said and started running.

We ran through agricultural fields. I took the shortest routes possible— sometimes that included running on a path, and sometimes straight through fields. I kept my pace steady, followed by the desperately dehydrated soldiers behind me.

All along the way, so long as we were within sight, an Israeli lookout followed our progress from a distance. They called us over the radio, saying we were going too fast and they were losing us. I nearly laughed out loud.

Suddenly, I saw a light straight ahead of us. I gauged the distance at about 100 yards. It was a farmer who'd taken to the field early. Without hesitation, I cut left into the field, ran 100 yards, and turned strongly to the right. The lookout informed us over the radio that there was something in front of us. We didn't bother answering. It was behind us already.

We kept running and came to a path. I looked behind me: everyone was running, the gaps were minimal. They were running like demons from hell, extracting the last reserves of strength from the deepest parts of their being: running and tripping, stabilizing and continuing, vomiting while running, leaning on their friends, and not stopping no matter what.

In the end of the film "Black Hawk Down," there's a scene where the Rangers are fleeing the city, vomiting as they are running. To this day, I get goosebumps watching that scene.

The night sky was getting brighter. It was astronomical dawn— the time when the sun is 18 degrees below the horizon— leaving us with mere minutes before daybreak. We reached the last line of hills and made a run for the last 800 yards before the river. Someone was using their head and sent out the younger teams, who were waiting in the ferries, to help us get through the final stretch. They reached us and took our packs from us. I burst out laughing when I saw some of my soldiers shoo them away, insisting to carry their packs all the way to the end.

I stopped before the Jordan River. The soldiers ran past me, and I counted them off. They crossed over a cable the younger teams had stretched between both sides of the river, and collapsed in the thicket on the opposite bank. Soldiers stripped them of their gear and helped them reach cover. I waited for the last of them to cross. I connected to the cable, and crossed the river. I didn't once look at the water torrents flowing beneath my feet. I was too tired to even think.

We agreed that if we got back at first light, we would wait on the bank so no one on the other side would be alerted. Despite that, I ordered my soldiers to board the jeeps. I rushed them, and instructed them to lie down in the vehicles. The officer in charge of the ferry tried to argue with me, but took one look at the intensity of my eyes and backed down. I got into one of the jeeps and lay down by the soldiers, so that even if someone on the other side spotted us, all they'd see were two jeeps without any soldiers on board. "Go!" I yelled at the driver.

Rocking along the dirt path ascending from the Jordan Valley, I looked at my soldiers. They were lying there dirty, ragged, pale as corpses—but with an unmistakable glimmer of pride in their eyes.

"You know, we have another operation up north in two weeks…" I joked.

"Take some other bunch of saps with you…" one soldier replied. We all burst out laughing, a feeling of relief settling over us.

We connected with the main road, then off to another dirt path heading towards to a makeshift camp specially erected for this operation. Medics helped the soldiers down; they were examined and hooked up to

IV infusions. I chased away the medic who approached me. Physically, there is no question my soldiers had gone through much worse than I had. My effort was down to holding back my nerves and making the right decisions. Sometimes commanders erroneously think that if they put in a shift like their subordinates, they will be setting a personal example. Nothing could be further from the truth: if I had lugged around the weight they'd carried, I could never have made clear-headed decisions— or, more accurately, adrenaline-infused decision, in this case compounded with the powerful Benzedrine pills…

The operations officer, my neighbor in the officers' quarters at the unit, came to congratulate me with a cold beer. We drank together. The alcohol and the Benzedrine, together with residual adrenaline, threw my systems into a tailspin— I was drunk in a matter of seconds. But it's all behind me now, I thought to myself. What a relief…

I was called over to the radio tent. The signaler yelled: "the army's Chief of Staff wants to talk to you." I was in trouble now: I wasn't sure I could even speak. I walked over to the phone, relieved to see it was the type where you had to hold down a button on the receiver for the other side to hear you. The Chief of Staff congratulated me on completing the operation, and thanked me. In the state I was in, I found that funny for some reason.

Luckily, I hadn't pressed the button, so he couldn't hear me laugh. But the radio officer turned pale…

"Now take care of the soldiers. I want each of them to get the full attention he deserves," he said. I managed to master out a yes sir, followed by an I'll see to it, sir.

I took another beer and lit a cigarette. I sat down on the food hamper, drank and smoked with pleasure. No one dared say anything. At that moment, I was as big as Mick Jagger. The second beer knocked me out, and I slept like a corpse.

Early the next morning, after some food, a shower, and a good night's sleep, we assembled in the briefing room for a debriefing.

I went up to the podium and described the events of the previous night in detail. There were many comments and insights, some humorous and others serious; but all in all, the mood was positive. We'd done it. At some point, the colonel I had walked out on at our meeting a couple of days prior commented: "You said you'd call it as you saw fit, and ended up doing just that."

"And it worked."

"Luckily for you…" he said.

I smiled, and someone shouted out: "And he's not a kibbutznik!" Everyone had a good laugh.

"Just a minute," the unit commander suddenly jumped

in, just as I was ready to go back to my seat.

The unit commander and the commander-in-chief stood at both my sides, removed my first lieutenant rank insignias, and replaced them with a captain's. When I left the briefing room, soldiers that had climbed up to the roof poured buckets of water over my head, as was customary, and hosed me down with a fire hose. It was a party.

The operations officer, my neighbor, said there was a surprise waiting for me in my room. I went to change into a dry uniform. In my room I found Tal, lying naked on my bed. Her smooth skin enticed me, her sexy bottom teased me… I ignored her, changed into dry clothes, and went back out to celebrate with the soldiers.

CHAPTER 15

AT THE FOOT OF MOUNT HERMON, 1981: A SENIOR TEAM

There comes a time you may find yourself torn between your unit commander and the Army High Command, forcing you to choose your allegiance. I faced that test on several occasions, not very successfully.

The early 1980s, the twilight of my service. The IDF was planning a large-scale operation to sweep south Lebanon clean. We felt like we had already played our part. We had recently completed a near-impossible walking operation, and felt we deserved a rest. But the army felt it was a shame to waste such a highly-trained team. So just like that, we found ourselves in battle procedures to secure an entrance route for tanks into south Lebanon.

The unit commander wanted nothing to do with the operation, but he had no choice. He sent me down to Northern Command with instructions to delay the operation for as long as I could. The operations officer and I drove up north. After a three-hour ride and a stop for falafel in Afula, we stopped and observed the axis I was supposed to walk that night. The terrain was hilly, you could almost call it a gorge, but I wasn't worried. In our physical condition, my soldiers and I could handle it. But there were Bedouins and farmers in the valleys beneath us—and where there were Bedouins, there were dogs.

When we turned to leave the lookout, the operations officer walking ahead of me suddenly halted, and I tripped over his leg. I tumbled all the way down the ridge. Luckily, the only serious injury I sustained was to my hand— an ugly, deep laceration. We wrapped it up in an impressive bandage and drove to Northern Command.

The command major-general and the division commander were present at the meeting. The major-general was an armored-corps man— he knew a thing or two about tanks, but not about walking night patrol. The division commander was a decorated paratrooper, who felt he knew all he needed to know on the subject. Keeping my unit commander's instructions in mind, I insisted it was impossible to carry out the patrol without being discovered. The division commander became upset.

"So we'll assign a paratrooper platoon if you can't do it," he barked.

"There's not a single soldier in the entire armed forces that can do what I do," I brazenly said.

I was a recently-promoted captain, facing off against a brigadier-general and a major-general. I was young, brash, and genuinely fearless. I enjoyed the confrontation.

The division commander introduced two officers who were to join us on the patrol, an engineering-corps officer and an armored-corps officer. I looked at them scornfully. The engineering-corps officer was ridiculously unfit for the assignment. The armored-corps officer was lean and athletic, but I highly doubted he could keep up with my team. The major-general asked the engineering-corps officer: "How's your fitness?"

"Excellent, sir. I run seven miles every day," he replied.

If he walks at all, it's probably from the office to the mess hall and back, I dismissively thought to myself. But the atmosphere was charged as it was, and I knew my opinion would not be welcomed. So I kept my mouth shut.

"And you?" the major-general asked the armored-corps officer.

"I'm decent, sir," he said. The understatement and confidence in his voice rendered his answer more credible.

"What do you say?" the major-general asked me.

"There's no way in hell they can do it," I said bluntly.

The division commander blew his top, raging about my arrogance and vanity, going on and on about paratroopers and reconnaissance units. I looked back at him indifferently, which made him all the more incensed. The major-general put an end to his rant, and informed me the operation will be going ahead, and that the two officers will be joining me.

"And if we're discovered?" I insisted.

"Are you certain you'll be discovered?" the major-general asked.

"On a clear-sky, moonlit night like tonight, with dogs and Bedouin all around, there's no way to not be discovered," I said.

"What are the consequences of being discovered?" he asked.

"I could kill whoever discovers us without making any noise. I could abduct them, but it would be hard to carry them back. Either way, we won't make it to the pass you want us to check. The question is, is that what you want?" I answered.

"What do you mean?"

"Do you want me to kill or abduct an innocent farmer on a path you want to keep secret?"

"No, I don't. Don't kill anyone and don't abduct

anyone," the major-general said.

We left the room frustrated. The order was to move ahead with preparations. Around evening time, my soldiers, who had spent the day preparing, arrived at the advanced post by the Lebanese border. I briefed them and inspected their gear before we left. I insisted the engineering-corps and armored-corps officers leave behind everything that wasn't absolutely essential. The armored-corps officer didn't argue. The engineering-corps officer insisted on taking his measuring instruments. I made him give it over to my soldiers, who griped about the extra weight but carried it nonetheless.

I placed the two officers in the middle of the force and made them remove their rank insignias, like I did. I appointed two of my soldiers to be in charge of the officers. I instructed the officers to do exactly as their appointed soldiers did at all times.

We sat waiting at the border for two more hours. With every passing moment, we grew increasingly irritable. It was clear that the later we left, the faster we'd have to walk, or even risk staying out in the field during daylight. As I usually did before an operation, I smoked a whole pack of cigarettes, my mouth pervaded with the dry taste of ash and smoke. Others were chewing on beef-jerky and exchanging harmless banter. Later, they decided to pick on the two officers. The engineering-cops officer tried to answer back, but was laughed out of town. The armored-corps officer smiled in silence.

Finally, the division commander arrived and said in an irritable voice that we had to leave immediately. I radioed command post, and they approved. I said we'd be calling it very close in terms of the time we had left at our disposal. They replied that there was no other choice, and to try to make it as far as we could. I realized it was a clash of egos. We were left with no choice. We headed out.

After such a long wait, the soldiers were off like a bat out of hell. I had to slow down their pace, which was ridiculous for such difficult terrain. The sector was clear of enemy forces, so we could walk without worrying about making noise. We climbed and descended, up and down, over and over. After about an hour, we had made up for the delay and were back on schedule. I checked up on the officers during the water break. The armored-corps officer seemed okay, but the engineering-corps officer was utterly spent, hunched over gasping for air. I asked how he was, and all he could muster was a faint nod. I figured he ran this whole time, because he didn't know how to walk at such a murderous pace. I was worried, but had no choice but to carry on.

Two hours later, I was informed the engineering-corps officer couldn't walk any further. This time, I took a twenty-minute break. I went over to see him: he was lying on his back, panting heavily. I tried to talk to him, but he was in no condition to answer. I had a problem on my hands. The whole point of the patrol was to observe and inspect the axis. I called the armored-corps officer over and asked for his opinion. He said that anything the engineering-corps officer could inspect, he was qualified to inspect as well, except for barrier-breaching, but he could probably do that as well.

I left the engineering-corps officer with two soldiers at a point I could later recognize between two boulders. I reported to command post, and was off again. I absolutely hated splintering forces. A couple of months prior, a squad of paratroopers had accidentally shot a splinter force— the whole army was still traumatized from the disaster. But, again, I had no choice.

We continued walking, going around the few houses sparsely scattered in the area. The dogs were barking, but we were a safe distance away. We slowed down our pace, and moved silently. A mere couple of weeks before, we'd walked a spitting-distance away from a Jordanian army sentinel without being spotted— we weren't sure what he'd seen, and he hadn't reacted anyway. I assumed we'd have room to maneuver here as well. An hour and a half later, we reached a pass we had identified in the aerial photos as the only possible place to cross. We observed the spot, and I couldn't believe my eyes: since that aerial photo was taken, more Bedouins had settled there, and the area was now dense and extremely difficult to cross. I started moving forward, and the dogs started barking. I decided to leave the force behind while I advanced together with two soldiers, Ami and Amir, carrying muffled rifles. There I was, forced to splinter the force again.

We snuck between the tents and the kennels. The dogs were barking like mad. We had almost crossed the hamlet when, out of nowhere, a dog pounced on us in rabid fury. Amir aimed well, and kicked him square in the head. The dog scampered away, whining. We heard a sound front the nearby tent. Someone was coming out, and we hurried to hide in the shadows. An Arab man emerged holding a shotgun and yelled: "Min hadha?" (Who's there?) He yelled two more times, and shot a round in the air. I held Amir back, whose finger was ready on the trigger. The man walked out to search for the intruder; Ami and Amir aimed their weapons at him, and I pulled out my combat knife. He turned around and looked directly at us. Our faces were darkened, and we were well-hidden in the long, dark shadows: the light of a full moon increases visibility, which is a bad thing, but the shadows it casts are deeper than the darkest of nights. Suddenly it hit me— my bandage was white, and was giving me away. I'd wanted to replace it before we left, but we had been in a hurry, and I couldn't find the time. The Bedouin raised his shotgun. I froze. I heard a muffled sound to my left, the sound of a muffled rifle going off. Both soldiers shot at almost exactly the same time. I saw the bullets hit his head, and he dropped like a stone. We ran over to grab him, and pulled him into the shadows. We waited in silence; the dogs barked, but that was all. I gestured to Ami, who quietly went over to spot where the Arab had hit the ground, turned over the blood-soaked earth and covered it with a large pile of goat dung.

Amir hoisted the dead Arab man over his shoulders, and we snuck back. We reached the rest of the force, who had in the meantime taken battle positions after hearing the muffled noises; they were almost inaudible, but to trained ears, they gave the story away. We quickly put some distance between ourselves and the hamlet, carrying the body with us. We stopped about 300 yards away, and I radioed into command post. After an irritatingly long wait, I was instructed to go on with the operation. I replied that was not an option, unless they wanted me to slaughter the entire hamlet. Besides, there wasn't enough time to make it to our objective and back. After another tense few moments, I was instructed to go back.

We opened a stretcher, loaded the body, and hastily started making our retreat. The way back was tough, an almost ceaseless steep ascent. The stretcher weighed us down, especially since we followed narrow winding goat trails, not wide enough to fit two people together. Thus, the soldiers had to carry the stretcher two at a time, instead of four. I was very proud of them. I tried not to walk too fast, but still, I wanted to reach the splinter force as soon as possible so we could make it back to the border before daybreak.

Halfway back, the armored-corps officer insisted he wanted to help carry the stretcher. I had been impressed by his walking abilities and how easily he fit in, so I agreed. But the soldiers refused to pass the stretcher—a matter of professional pride. He didn't insist, and I stayed out of it.

We reached the splinter force. The engineering-corps officer was paralyzed with cramps; he could hardly move, let alone walk. We unloaded the corpse, and loaded the officer in its stead. We reached the border before daybreak.

When we reached the fence, the division commander was waiting for us, incandescent with rage.

"You just wait, I'm not finished with you!" he screamed at me. "I'll personally see to it that you're never promoted again. You'll remain a captain for the rest of your life!"

I looked him square in the eye and said in a soft voice: "I'm discharging next week. You can stop my promotion in South America." I kept walking, my soldiers following close behind, stifling their giggles.

CHAPTER 16

LEBANON-SINAI-LEBANON, 1981: AN OFFICERS' OPERATION

There was a period when we carried out ambushes or attacks in Lebanon on an almost weekly basis. These operations were simple and rapidly executed, but not always very effective. For us, however, they provided invaluable operational experience.

Tal left me. She finished her service, enrolled in college, and decided in the spur of the moment to volunteer at a field school in Sharm El Sheikh, the most southerly point of the Sinai Peninsula.

I was a captain, a seasoned soldier. And as I've already mentioned, being an officer in the unit went a long way towards helping you with the ladies. I had a thing going on with a girl from one of the auxiliary units, but it wasn't going anywhere.

During lunch one day, someone asked me if I was taking part in the officers' operation. I said of course I was, but I actually had no idea what he was talking about... I ran as quick as I could to the company commander and harangued him to assign me to this operation. I didn't even know what the operation was.

The company commander said that the roster was full, but he'd see what he could do. I kept nagging and, just to get rid of me, he agreed to put me on the stand-in list. Every operation had stand-ins, in case something happened to one of the participants.

From there, I went straight to the unit commander to complain that the company commander was excluding me. He promised he'd talk to him. I couldn't keep bugging him because he was busy— he was the unit commander, after all— so I got his secretary to agree to bring my name up every half hour. Eventually I went to the administrative adjutant and simply put my name down on the operations list. While at the office, I tried to call Tal at Sharm El Sheikh, but the line was dead. The adjutant promised to let me know as soon as it was up again.

I went to sign for equipment, but was rebuffed and told my name wasn't on the list. I went back to the company commander, he promised it would be fine. I put on trainers and went out to exercise. By evening-time, I still wasn't able to get through to Tal, nor did I receive a decisive answer from the company commander. I went to the club to play bridge with my soldiers, and didn't do very well.

The next morning, I saw the unit commander in the mess hall during breakfast. I told him that if I wasn't going to be part of the operation, I'd be discharging. He was hardly bothered. So I went to the adjutant and asked to formally begin the discharging process. Fifteen minutes later, I was called into the office. I'd done it, they assigned me to the operation!

An ambush in Lebanon. Great. I signed for equipment and joined the battle procedure. An officers' operation is fun— you get to be a regular soldier again, without the headache of bearing all the responsibility.

I still couldn't get through to Sharm El Sheikh. The countdown to the operation had begun; we were departing in ten hours. I was given a seemingly-ordinary radio, which was in fact filled with powerful explosives, a classic booby-trap. After that, it was briefing, roll call, schematic model, and rest. I never understood how anyone could rest with adrenaline pumping through their veins.

Finally, I got hold of the field school in Sharm El Sheikh. Tal wasn't there, so someone went looking for her. By the time she got back to the field school, whenever that was, the line was dead already. How is it that an army can carry out covert overseas operations with pinpoint precision but can't maintain one goddamn telephone line? Not long after, though, I managed to reach her. She said she was happy, and that everything was great. I tried to hint that I was going on an operation without explicitly saying so, but she didn't seem very interested. We said goodbye.

There were two hours left before departure. I opened a pack of cigarette and chain-smoked my way through it. Thirty minutes before takeoff, we sat waiting in formation until the helicopters finally arrived. Walking down to the runway with your equipment on your back imbues you with a feeling of elation. You're ready, you're fit, you have the best equipment, your clothes are still dry and your stomach is still full. You feel like a predator about to go out on a hunt; you look around you, surrounded by the other lions of the pack, geared and ready for action.

The Twin Two-Twelve (Bell 212 helicopter) reeked of burned fuel and grease. We took off into the night, two choppers packed with battle-hardened, amped-up officers. We landed in Lebanon in pitch darkness. We fell into formation and started walking. It felt a bit weird to be in the middle of the file rather than leading its front; not being the one to call the shots, simply walking in formation.

After a couple of minutes of walking, you start sweating. Slowly, your body gets soaked; a couple of minutes later, your face is so awash with sweat that you don't even bother wiping it off anymore. When breaks come, you are as grateful as any common soldier, guzzling down water in huge gulps. Without question, the water in those old, moldy canteens is the best water in the world.

After three hours of walking, we reached a road. We spread out to set the ambush, and waited. A light breeze dried the sweat off our bodies, and within a few minutes, it started getting cold. We waited and waited, but whatever was supposed to come didn't (we weren't even sure what it was). There were feverish discussions going on over the radio, but I was just a simple soldier in this operation, so I was strictly out of the loop. In the meantime, I tore the shoulder-straps off the booby-trap radio and placed it in between the rocks, to make it seem as though it was abandoned in haste.

We received an order to be prepared. They said the next car was the car we'd been waiting for. A truck with colorful headlights made its way up the hill. This couldn't possibly be it, I thought to myself. But then the order came: "On my command, open fire!"

The truck drove straight into the ambush. I could clearly make out the driver in the cabin dozily smoking a cigarette with an open window. The command to fire came, and the night erupted into a cacophony of assault rifle fire and anti-tank LAW rockets. Two rockets hit the truck cabin. "Grenade!" one of the officers yelled, and tossed a grenade under the truck which detonated and blew up the gas tank. The truck was ablaze, a flaming hunk of metal; the driver was leaned over the wheel, burned to a blackened crisp, the weight of his body honking the car horn. Two additional LAW rockets didn't resolve the issue.

We left as quickly as we could. Needless to say, I left the booby-trapped radio behind. We retreated like scared kids caught red-handed. A jeep full of enemy soldiers quickly arrived at the scene, and started firing everywhere with a Soviet DShK 1938 heavy machine gun. The rounds went well over our heads, as we were down in the canyon by then. I received a spontaneous order to stay behind with two other officers and form a rear guard.

We lay between the huge boulders, looking up and scanning the descent down to the canyon. I checked my ammunition: I had five magazines left, I had only shot two. I also had a couple of grenades left. Some figures appeared on the horizon, we picked them off with precision using our scopes. Two hit the ground, the rest dispersed. We couldn't see a thing in the dark. We shot in their general direction for deterrence, but there was no return fire.

We heard the sound of approaching helicopters. A round was shot in our direction, we fired back. The helicopters descended into the canyon from its far side. The two other soldiers and I suddenly realized we were a fair distance away. We shouted to one another and made a run for the makeshift landing pad. We ran across the canyon with full gear in pitch-black. We tripped, we fell, we hit the stones on the ground, but we kept on running. When we came within 100 yards of the landing pad, we saw one of the helicopters taking off and flying away. Some more rounds were shot, again missing their target. We kept on running. By the time we reached the landing pad, it was abandoned.

We looked around at each other, petrified. We were alone, three officers in the heart of enemy territory. They had forgotten us, or left us behind to pull the main force out. As far as we were concerned, it made no difference. Above us, at the mouth of the canyon, we could hear shouting and gunfire. The terrorists were revving themselves up before descending into the canyon.

Further down the canyon, about three miles down, there was another possible landing spot. None of us had a radio with us. We decided to run for it. Normally, three miles of open terrain was a piece of cake for us, but running downhill in a rocky, thorny, pitch-black canyon was an utter nightmare. Our throats closed up, our breaths grew shorter, we sweated bullets; we expected to feel bullets piercing our backs at any moment. We ran as if we were possessed. I hit a stone, tumbled over and fell, got up and kept running. My knee hurt, as did my elbow. I kept running. We realized we had passed the landing spot, because we suddenly found ourselves standing at the edge of a precipice. We stopped in our tracks, panting heavily, and headed back at a slower pace. We reached a crossing between two canyons — but it was too narrow for a helicopter to land. We sat down on a rock, completely out of ideas. We drank some more water. The shouting behind us was getting closer. We assumed we had no more than an hour before they reached us. We turned on our homing devices, and waited.

Maybe they just forgot about us. I'm not getting captured, I thought to myself. I'll save the last bullet for myself, just in case. Maybe a grenade is better, actually. With a bullet, I might miss. Yes, a grenade is better. But we'll give them hell first. I examined my ammunition. My magazine was dented, probably from the fall a couple of minutes earlier. I changed it for a new one. I'd lost a grenade too, but still had one left. The shouting was getting closer and closer.

And then we suddenly heard the sound of helicopter rotors approaching. A sweet, sweet sound— like your

mother calling you to the dinner table. The two helicopters came in low behind us, and to our astonishment
they flew right above our heads and past us. We shouted
as loud as we could, turned on our flashlights, but nothing. "Those were Cobras," one of the soldiers said.

"Right," we said with a sigh of relief.

The choppers stabilized in the air, and laid down a
carpet of fire over the rest of the canyon. The Cobra
minigun sounds like demons out of hell, but for once—
those demons were on our side. A Twin Two-Twelve
arrived and shone a spotlight down; when it saw it had
nowhere to land, it hovered as close to the ground as it
could. One by one, we climbed onto its skids and the
flight mechanic pulled us into the cabin. We took off
and flew back home.

The debriefing started early the next morning. I
wasn't really listening; I was busy thinking about an
odd and enticing message Tal had left with the unit
telephone operator. The only moment I was stirred
back into attention was when someone mentioned that
the booby-trapped radio had been taken back to the
headquarters of the terrorist organization in Tyre, where
it later detonated and razed the place to the ground. I
have since bragged that I singlehandedly thwarted that
organization.

As soon as the debriefing was done, I went to the

administrative company commander and asked to take out a car from the motor pool for three days. The only one they had for me was a Dodge D200, a semi-truck. I took it. That afternoon, I headed south. By 10 PM, I had reached Eilat; for the rest of the night, I was driving southbound down the Sinai coastal highway, along the shores of the Red Sea.

I smoked a cigarette. The window was cracked open, and I was feeling drowsy. Suddenly I became convinced a group of Saudi Arabian soldiers had crossed the bay and set up an ambush for me. I shook my head and tried to focus on the road. But what if there really was an ambush? I drove on, fully alert now, but couldn't shake off the fear. In Nuweiba, I stopped to get a couple of hours' sleep. Later the following morning, I made it to Sharm El Sheikh.

"Where is she?" I asked. No one was really certain. Finally, someone suggested she might be at the secluded beach. I got some directions and headed there. After scaling the last line of bounders before the sea, I discovered a beautiful, tiny secluded beach. Tal was sitting there, completely naked, looking out at the sea.

I snuck up behind her and hugged her. She tried to turn around, but I wouldn't let her. She struggled, but I easily overpowered her. She growled like a beast. Finally, she stopped resisting. I kissed the back of her neck, her body quivered. My hands roamed all over her body, caressing, grabbing, petting, squeezing… Our breaths grew shorter.

When everything was done, I got back in the truck and drove home, still on the lookout for ambushes. There were none. To this day, when I drive at night, I look out for ambushes. More often than not, there are none…

CHAPTER 17

EREZ, TAL, AND EITAN'S STORY

Tal enlisted a short while after Erez's team did, and discharged a short while before them.

When Tal was little, her nickname was Tiltul. As she got older, she grew to resent the name. For years, she tried in vain to shake off that childish nickname. When she was six years old, her parents relocated to Africa. Her father was a project manager at Solel Boneh, one of the largest construction and civil engineering companies in Israel. They lived in a large house, waited on by servants. Tal attended an American school; she liked the school, and the school liked her.

Tal loved Africa. She loved the heat, the people, taking trips with her family in the great national parks, and the animals. She was one sister sandwiched between two brothers, and she acted as if she were the third brother.

They had their own games that they invented, a tree-house, and a gardener who taught them the secrets of nature.

When Tal was eleven years old, her family returned home to Kfar Saba, a small city near Tel-Aviv. She had a hard time: she was tall and awkward, and had the mannerisms of a white girl in Africa. She found herself constantly looking for the black cook and cleaner. Her English was good, but she made terrible grammatical errors in Hebrew, especially in writing. She didn't fit in socially, and would often come home in tears. Her brothers, who also had a hard time at first, managed to fit in by excelling at sports. Not long after the family's return to Israel, the Yom Kippur War broke out, plunging the country into despair; grief and loss pervaded every city and settlement. In that social climate, no one had any time for Tal's difficulties.

The next few years saw two processes that would change her life completely: she grew out of puberty and emerged a tall, beautiful young girl. Her body stabilized, and became feminine. The second process saw her father becoming a successful and very wealthy private contractor. They moved into a fancy house; she owned every ostentatious thing one could possibly want.

Boys sought her attention, and girls followed suit. Almost at once, Tal metamorphosed from an "ugly duckling" into a beautiful and popular girl. Almost inevitably, Tal became vain and arrogant. Her relationship with boys grew increasingly asymmetrical, with her calling the shots like a queen bee.

When she was sixteen years and two months old, Tal was raped. It happened almost by accident. She was at a beach party, and a guy she didn't know took her to a dark, secluded spot. She was a bit intoxicated, and delighted by the stranger's courtship. He kissed her and tried to touch her body; when she refused, he pounced on her, beat her, and brutally raped her. Tal tried to fight back, but was stunned by his aggression. She froze up completely. She felt like she had been hurled into another world, into hell. A world where she didn't know the rules and didn't know what to do. When he finished, he left her there crying and disappeared.

Tal had a hard time settling back into her normal life. She couldn't shake the feeling of humiliation and helplessness. She didn't tell a soul about what had happened. She felt guilty without quite knowing why. Her social life slowly withered away, and was suffused with suspicion. Her studies deteriorated. She felt detached and defiled.

The rapist's anonymity made him a monster in her mind. She hadn't known who he was before, and she never saw him again. Nor did she have an easy way to find out who he was. For those reasons, she could imagine that maybe the whole thing never even happened; she latched onto that notion. Slowly but surely, Tal pulled herself out of the abyss: she started going out again. Her relationships with the opposite sex became aggressive— she took what she wanted and made sure to give nothing in return. She let her family spoil her, lavish her with attention and gifts. They sensed that something had happened, but didn't know what.

A while later, she decided that since she was no longer a virgin anyway, she might as well explore the world of sex. She gave herself to a slew of boys and men, and increasingly started to enjoy herself as well. She had many lovers— some were utterly useless, some were not bad, and some truly taught her about pleasure.

She started taking martial arts lessons and dedicated herself fully. At the age of seventeen, she got a nose job, adjusting her physical appearance to complement her style. When she got her driver's license, her father bought her a red sports car. Kids her age were intimidated by her, so she befriended older boys and girls. Her interests became increasingly superficial, to the point of nonexistence.

She graduated high school a mediocre student, well below her actual potential, but she couldn't have cared less. In fact, she didn't care about anything. Then, one hot afternoon, she filled a tub full of water, crawled in, and cut the veins of her left wrist.

Her mother found her on the brink of death. She was rushed to the hospital, got emergency treatment, and made it out alive. Her perturbed and scared parents sent her to see a psychologist. The psychologist, a young man, allowed her to seduce him, thinking it would help her. Tal decided it was a waste of her time and quit therapy.

Her parents then hired a well-known female psychologist, but her relationship with Tal became heated and contentious. The psychologist, in a decidedly unprofessional move, recommended psychiatric treatment and prescription drugs. No one touched the heart of the problem. Tal refused to reveal she had been raped.

And then she met Eitan on the beach, by chance. She was sitting with a friend, and Eitan was sitting not far away from them. When two guys started pestering the girls, Eitan came over and sat next to them, driving the two guys away. Tal thanked him and teased him, telling him he did it only so that he could get closer to them himself. Eitan was a bit offended and clammed up. Tal found that cute.

When they left, Eitan gathered up the courage and asked her out to a movie. He offered to pick her up— she told him that she would pick him up. That evening, she rolled up in her red sports car, and the two went to see the musical "Hair." They agreed it was a fun movie with a sad ending. They loved the irreverence and rebelliousness of the movie's protagonists, so far removed from their own lives.

Later, they sat in a teahouse, the type that had been popping up like mushrooms after rain at that time. They talked for hours, and Tal felt like she could tell him anything. She spoke about her childhood, about Africa, and how hard it was to return. He told her that he had also been to Africa with his father, who was later killed as a soldier during the Yom Kippur War; he talked about grief and loss, and about his mother and brother.

He seemed uniquely vulnerable to her, yet not at all sorry and miserable. He had an optimism and good will about him which conveyed calm, despite his large proportions. Eitan was tall and muscular, like a figure from Greek mythology.

At the end of the evening, they kissed goodbye. For the first time in years, she felt truly alive. She wanted to throw herself in his arms. She did exactly that when they next met, at the beach. She later made him swim naked with her at night. They met again, and slept together on their third date. He told her innocently that it was his first time. For some reason, that struck a chord deep inside her. Despite Eitan's inexperience, the sex was fulfilling. They met almost every day. Tal thought she might be in love.

Eitan was big, strong, loyal, and affectionate. Tal welcomed the change with open arms. And then he told her he was enlisting to a top-secret elite unit. Tal didn't like the idea that he'd be leaving her and that she'd only see him occasionally on weekends. But he refused to give it a second thought.

They desperately tried to wring the last drop out of the time they had left together. Inevitably, though, the day finally came when Tal drove Eitan to the recruiting office. She didn't cry; she hugged him and kissed him, and drove home. That same day, she comforted herself in the arms of another male friend. She was angry and felt betrayed and did what she always did: ruined everything. She told herself that was what she deserved. When Eitan first came home for the weekend, she told him it was over. She wasn't one to wait.

The process of her enlistment went on uninterrupted. The Ministry of Health hadn't updated the army on the issue of her mental health; a cog in the bureaucratic machine was broken, and Tal enlisted before the army received any such information. She was looking forward to her military service, which she saw as an opportunity to start off with a clean slate. She was desperate to be stationed in the special unit Eitan was serving in. She called on every connection she had: her father, Eitan's mother— who was well-known in the army, since her late husband had been a popular and beloved officer before his death— and through another cousin, as well.

She enlisted, and managed to get through boot camp. She then got her wish, and was stationed to serve in Eitan's unit. In the meantime, the systems finally synched up, and the army discovered she had an attempted suicide to her name. Due to the sensitive nature of her position, her mental health could be an issue; the army had a tough call to make. She was sent home and instructed to await their decision.

Tal celebrated being free and home again, even if only temporarily. She went to see her old psychologist, and made her write a letter confirming she was no longer a threat to herself.

The army caved, and she went on to serve in the unit. Eitan was there, undergoing a qualification course, the period of time soldiers are at their absolute least accessible. They worked their socks off day and night, and by the time the weekend arrived all they wanted was sleep. Eitan was a cadet in the team led by Erez— a certified nutjob, standing out even in such an extreme environment. So Tal hardly saw him, and even on the rare occasions she did, they hardly spoke.

Tal had two affairs during this period: one was a short-lived fling with a senior-ranking married officer, and the other with a veteran combatant. After serving in the unit for a year, Tal ran into Eitan at a party at home over the weekend. Eitan had just completed one of the least taxing weeks in the qualification course, and was very energetic. He was the center of attention, encircled by friends and acquaintances who tried to squeeze any bit of information from him about the special, secret unit. He kidded around with everyone, but divulged nothing. At the end of the evening, Tal took him to her house without saying anything, and the two spent the night making passionate, desperate love. Eitan then fell asleep and Tal went out to the kitchen, where she ran into her mother.

"I thought I heard Eitan's voice before," her mother said.

"Yeah, it's him. But he's asleep already," Tal replied.

"Tal, don't do this to him again…"

"Do what?" Tal asked incredulously.

"Break his heart," her mother replied. "Love him, dump him, torture him… He doesn't deserve that."

"And what do I deserve, Mom? Do I deserve a guy who doesn't have any time for me? A guy who prefers his team over me? Is that what I deserve?"

"You deserve everything, Tiltul. But you already have everything. He has nothing."

"Mom, you have no idea what I do or do not have."

"Yes, I've come to understand that, dear. But maybe, just this once, do what's right for you too, and stay with him."

"I can't, Mom. A soldier in training is not a human being, he's a warrior on a production line. Maybe one day, after the qualification course…"

"It pains me to see this, Tiltul. It hurts me to see both of you like this."

"Me too, Mom. More than you know," Tal concluded.

Tal woke Eitan up in the morning, fixed him breakfast, and took him home. She didn't respond to his attempts to meet up later. The following day, she saw him during the usual Sunday fitness session—a killer workout that every combatant, cadet, and officer undertook every Sunday. The girls would settle in and enjoy watching the ripped, half-naked young men busting their asses in an extreme strenuous workout. They were dripping wet, their muscles bulging; they were truly a sight to behold.

Erez's team always trained apart from the rest of the unit, with additional exertions like 2,000 sit-ups—because Erez's girlfriend despised pot-bellies— or a couple of extra rounds of climbing a rope using only their arms— because Team Erez needed to be able to lift cars.

Tal knew the car story. Everybody knew it. Team Erez had been driving in Tel-Aviv and entered a narrow street with the army truck. Cars were parked on both sides of the street and there was no way through. Erez ordered the team off the truck, and they went car by car, lifting them up from where they were parked and placing them on the sidewalk. Near the end, there was a couple inside one of the cars. The man, after being hoisted into the air inside the car and being unceremoniously placed on the curb, leaped out of the car in anger, ready to fight. His face turned when he saw the burly bunch of young men facing him. He tried to protest anyway, but Erez asked him a question which immediately became enshrined in unit folklore: "Hey, buddy, can't you count?"

Eitan stood out in all departments, certainly in fitness training. He was big, almost 6'5, but unlike most large men, he had a lean frame. So he could leverage his body with explosive propulsion. Everything was easier for Eitan. Sunday fitness session had an audience, but Tal broke ranks and returned to the radio room. She didn't renew her relationship with Eitan, and he stopped trying. He had his qualification course to think about.

Upon completing his course, Eitan was sent to officer training. Tal still refused to see him. She considered his going to officer training a form of betrayal: an officer in the unit had to sign a two-year extension to his service, and the job was demanding. Tal was adamant she deserved someone's undivided attention.

To everyone shock and the unit commander's disappointment, at the end of officer training Eitan chose to remain as a course commander and train the next batch of cadets rather than return to the unit. The unit sent Erez out to talk to him about his decision, but when he came back, the only thing he said was: "We decided he's going to stay there."

The senior command of the unit was incensed, but nothing could change Eitan's mind. Later, Eitan took a command role in the paratrooper corps, and never returned to the unit.

Tal was angry. She wanted to leave, but she didn't have a lot of time left to serve anyway, so she decided to stick it out. She eyed the unit doctor, who was older than the others and seemed smarter as well. But then, one day, Erez burst half-naked into the radio room and forced her to call half the army in search of a soldier who might have gone missing beyond the border.

He was upset, and she found that arousing. She teased him, and saw that despite the stress he was under, Erez responded to her advances. After the soldier was found safe and well, she kept Erez in the radio room. He was aggressive— almost violent— in stark contrast to Eitan's gentle strength. She was awash with guilt, but let herself get swept away.

Erez had just returned from a failed operation, so he was guaranteed to have time for her. The attention he gave her was neither lavish nor too considerate, but Tal enjoyed it. She enjoyed the slight sting of humiliation in having to seek him out, all the while knowing she could easily find him and draw him into her world. She derived pleasure from their shared guilt, even though she knew she was damaging their team solidarity: she knew the soldiers, Eitan's friends, were angry. She also knew someone must have told Eitan about their affair.

So it went on for a couple of weeks, until Erez was finally assigned an operation. His dedication was absolute. He had forgotten Tal even existed, and wouldn't set any time aside for her under any condition. One Friday, she offered Erez to come to her house— but he chose to stay in the unit instead and study axes of advance.

Tal was mad. And when Tal was mad, she did what she always did: start a new affair. The doctor fell prey to her advances without much resistance. Even though he was pretty disappointing in bed, she kept the affair going. Tal expected Erez to notice, but his mind was solely on the operation— until he walked in on them making out, half naked in the infirmary. Still, his reaction irritated her: Erez waited for them to get dressed, and then went straight for the doctor and berated him for skipping practice.

She did all she could to penetrate Erez's hard exterior, to no avail. The doctor wouldn't see her anymore, but that was fine by her. Erez returned from the operation with the aura of a hero, and still refused to see her.

He was pleased to have a pretense to end things with Tal. Even though he liked her and found her very attractive, from day one their relationship had been stained with guilt. Erez knew how deeply Eitan felt about Tal, and every time he was with her, he felt he was stabbing a dear friend in the back. Erez had almost paternal feelings towards Eitan, and had reached the conclusion that Tal and Eitan should be together. At first, Erez thought refusing to see Tal would send her back to Eitan's arms. Later, though, he realized a girl like Tal simply relished the challenge of breaking his resistance. So he started speaking with her again. Erez told her that she and Eitan had to be together, that she might be attracted to him—but that she loved Eitan.

Tal couldn't believe someone was breaking up with her. Over the years, she had taken pains to always be the one to leave, so she wouldn't be in a position to get hurt. At first, she was offended, but then she realized he was moving aside to make room for Eitan. She realized she could never be with Eitan until she let go of whatever emotions she had for Erez. Then she came up with a creative idea: what if she tied the rape and humiliation that she had experienced to her relationship with Erez? That way she would be rid both of him and the terrible memories at once… Bind humiliation to humiliation and be rid of both.

Once she made up her mind, she started actively pursuing it. First, she cut all ties with Erez, and then sent him hints and subtle provocations she was sure were driving him mad.

Her service came to an end, and she discharged with no regrets. She sent Erez a letter, saying that if he slept with her just one more time, she'd go back to Eitan. And then she went to volunteer at the field school in Sharm El Sheikh.

Erez obsessively tried to reach her. She wasn't avoiding him, she was just hard to reach. At last, after countless attempts on his part, she finally called him and left a message that she was waiting for him— but that he had to surprise her and pretend to rape her. The shocked operator who took the message asked her to repeat it three times, to make sure she had heard correctly, but since she remembered Tal from her time at the unit, she conveyed the message word for word.

Tal didn't have to wait long. Two days later, when she went swimming naked at her secret beach, Erez arrived. She didn't hear him approaching, but when he grabbed her from behind, she recognized his scent and the powerful hands subduing her. She resisted, but not too much. She let herself be conquered, but this time decided to enjoy it. She felt like a primordial woman, forcefully taken by the strongest male in her tribe. He became gentler, and she slapped him in the face. Erez laughed and kissed her long and tender. He said only one thing: "You promised you'd go back to him after this."

He put his clothes back on, got into that ridiculously oversized Dodge D200, and drove away.

Two weeks later, Tal left the field school and returned home. She looked for Eitan until she finally found him. She courted him relentlessly, until he finally agreed to take her back. She was a loyal partner. She waited for him to come home on weekends and gave him all the love and warmth he needed. They talked about Erez: at first, Eitan felt jealousy, which then morphed into pain and hurt. But once he became truly convinced Tal was his for good, he made his peace with what had happened.

Tal got into medical school, and Eitan went on to become the youngest regiment commander in the army. Eitan and Tal got married, and Erez, along with the rest of the team, celebrated with them. Over the following years, they met Erez several times. They were even invited to his wedding, but they never became close friends.

Twenty years later, when she was on duty at the

hospital one day, wounded people from a terrorist attack started flooding into the emergency room. There was almost nothing she could do for any of them. Tal noticed two young, lacerated and disfigured children. When she got closer, she recognized the girl. It was Erez's daughter.

She later saw Lauren, and wouldn't let her go near the bodies. Erez came too that afternoon, worn and weary. He was half a man. Tal looked him in the eyes, but all she could see was despair.

When she told Eitan, he didn't say a word. She saw that look in his eyes she had only seen before on rare occasions. Eitan wanted to scream. Tal tried to reach out to him, but he withdrew. She could see he was burning with rage inside.

Tal asked him to take Erez back into service. Eitan said he didn't know.

"Eitan, it's the only thing that could bring him back to life…"

CHAPTER 18

RAIN: RESERVE DUTY IN LEBANON

Erez discharged along with his team, even though he was asked to stay in the service. But he had run out of steam, and wasn't interested in commanding a broader framework at that stage in his life. After discharging, he joined the Israel Security Agency as a security guard— a role necessitating minimal interaction. At the same time, he returned to reserve duty in the mid-80s.

Reserve duty for combatants can be a hazardous affair, especially during the first years. On the one hand, they are seasoned and experienced soldiers, but their bodies and physical fitness are not the same as they were when they trained regularly. Furthermore, they are now civilians, not soldiers; taking orders for a civilian is not the same for a soldier in regular service. Both commanders and soldiers must adjust to this new

**situation. Making these adjustments is by no means
easy, and— considering the challenges they face— can
lead to disaster.**

Two years after discharging, I was called up for the first
time to reserve duty in Lebanon. I was abroad during
the two years that had lapsed. Some of my soldiers had
taken part in a controversial war. Frameworks had been
dismantled and reconfigured. We were reassembled as
a team and annexed to a company of veteran soldiers.

During the first week of training, I felt there was some
rust in the gears. A defining trait of our regular service
was the team's rapid and blind compliance with orders
during operations. When we were off-duty, they could
say anything and laugh at my expense as they pleased,
but in action— they followed my orders decisively. Now,
however, I saw for the first time looks of reluctance on
their faces and hesitation in their execution. In combat
or in training, my orders were clear and sharp, and the
team always responded immediately. Over time, some
orders became so ingrained in their habits that there
was no need to even say them out loud— a slight nod of
the head or a pointed finger were enough. But in reserve
duty, everything had to be said— often more than once.

I sat on a rock in frustration after another mediocre warfare exercise. The soldiers walked right past me,

joking among themselves. I lit a cigarette, trying to think what was going wrong. The company commander, Yossi Ron, a legendary figure in the unit and ten years older than us, sat next to me. Usually, officers and commanders kept their thoughts to themselves due to the competitive nature of the unit; but Yossi and I weren't in competition, so I told him what was bothering me.

"It's simple," he replied, "keep your distance from them."

"But I was always very close to them, and it always worked."

"They worshipped you then, but that's over now."

"But they need the closeness…"

"No, they don't. You're the one who needs it," he said. "You need to get over it, fast."

He patted me on the back and went to get a cup of coffee brewed on an open fire by a group of senior soldiers, who had essentially come to reserve duty for the coffee. I observed the way Yossi conducted himself. He was amicable, but he wasn't their friend. It was clear he was the commander.

We drove up to Lebanon in a battered civilian truck. The army had advanced since the days of the D500. I sat up front, putting some distance between myself and the rest of the team. I read a book and chatted with the driver. It was one of the most boring drives I've ever been on— and coming from someone who was making his living in airplane security, that's saying something.

We crossed the border, clutching our rifles close to our chests. After about an hour, we reached our destination: Nabatieh, a medium-sized town with multiple-story houses scattered across a range of hills, with an utterly-obliterated road infrastructure and plenty of open spaces. We settled in a semi-demolished two-story building south of the town. A lookout was set up on the top floor, while the main floor housed the operations room, kitchen, mess-hall, and administrative sleeping quarters. The ground floor had a basement and housed the soldiers' sleeping quarters. A field shower and latrine were installed outside. In line with my new approach, I set up in the administrative sleeping quarters. I went to the operations room to study the terrain.

Our first assignment was a presence patrol. I went up to the lookout and perused the map and aerial photos. I called the team up, and explained the axis we would be taking. They then went to prepare their gear. During roll call, I was more meticulous than ever, making sure they didn't take anything with them that wasn't strictly essential: just their combat vests, magazines, two regular grenades and one smoke grenade, canteens, field knifes, and nothing else. I wanted them light and nimble. Veteran soldiers tend to pack everything they suspect they might possibly need, from food to climbing gear.

We were off. I led them through the fence. The road was the likeliest place to face an ambush. We went down through the field, walking in a formation of two wide-ly-dispersed squads in front and a third squad securing the rear. We weren't used to this formation: we were night creatures, reared and raised on a gradient-line or two-file formation. The sky was cloudy, but it wasn't raining. Typical Lebanese fall. I was walking in the middle with the radio, and quickly realized that I was quite conspicuously the one in charge— and thus, the prime target— but I remained in that spot, which had the best command of the field.

Autumn in Lebanon— the fields are brown and the vegetation is thorny. I walked slowly, allowing our senses to attune to the environment. We descended down a long, inclined field, crossed the main road, and entered the town. We heard a sound, loud and clear: Click… Our heightened senses immediately realized that was the sound of a lever disconnecting from a hand grenade.

"Grenade!" I shouted and threw myself to the ground. The soldiers reacted each at his own pace, but soon enough we were all on the ground. "21, 22, 23, 24…" Nothing. I counted five more seconds, as a safety measure. I got up to look for enemy forces, but found none. About three yards away I saw a lemon-shaped Soviet F1 grenade— a limonka— completely intact.

"Circumferential defense," I commanded. To my relief, the order was carried out quickly and efficiently.

"Look for the thrower, but do not pursue," command post said over the radio.

I looked around, spotting groups of people here and there, including a bunch of kids in school uniforms. I reported over the radio. I was instructed to look for the thrower and then continue. I decided not to look— it seemed impractical. I cleared the area, stepped back, aimed my rifle, and fired. My Colt AR-15 was finely tuned after a week of practice, and on the third shot, the grenade exploded safely. We got our stuff together, and moved on. This was clearly an intentional warm welcome.

We continued into the town, walking in two files on either side of the street— a formation we were more comfortable with, but which made it more difficult to command the area. The street reacted to us with clear detestation, but no hostility yet. After another hour, I called a break. We entered a building, went up to the roof, and rested. A couple of minutes later, dissent started.

"Why here?" one soldier said.

"Why not?" I replied.

"We're sitting ducks here."

"I don't think so. We've got high ground, overlooking the whole area."

"But we're sticking out," he insisted.

"No one will see us if they're not looking up."

"Or if they saw us coming in."

"Yes, but the rule of arbitrariness is important."

"The what?"

"Rule of arbitrariness. Choose arbitrarily, don't repeat the same action, and apply different logics to every decision you make. That way, no one can predict your next move," I explained.

The next time we stopped, on the roof of a different apartment building, a mother with three children came up carrying a tray with cups of coffee.

"Thank them, but don't drink it," I said sharply.

"Why?" Yoni asked.

I didn't answer. Yoni took a cup of coffee and sipped it defiantly. He looked at me and said: "Drink up, boys. Why are you not drinking? The coffee's good." The soldiers all turned and looked at me.

"Yoni, put down the cup," I said quietly, instead of cocking my rifle…

Hearing my grave tone of voice, he set down the cup.

"Unload your weapon," I said as I stood up and towered over him.

"Why?"

I didn't answer. I extended my arm forward and opened my palm, waiting for his magazine. He unloaded his weapon and handed me the magazine.

"You're not a soldier anymore," I told him. He snickered, but no one joined him.

We continued the patrol. It was hard to stay alert: I walked slowly, and stopped wherever I felt we weren't in immediate danger.

The ascent back to our post felt good— too good. I could feel the soldiers' discipline slipping. I stopped, and reminded them of the dangers we were facing. I explained that most accidents happened within two miles of the destination.

The following day, before going out on patrol, I told them the place was dangerous.

"There are people here who want to harm us. This mission itself is meaningless, but it needs to be done. As far as I'm concerned, our mission is to get out of here unharmed. We will use every precaution, and react incisively and aggressively to the slightest sign of danger. The only way to do that is to be soldiers," I told them. "If you can't follow orders, you're not a soldier," I stopped and turned to Yoni.

"Yoni, you're not coming out with us. You're on kitchen duty," I informed him.

"W-What are you talking about? I'll report you! I-I…" he stuttered.

I didn't answer. "Roll call outside in five minutes," I said.

When we assembled outside, Yoni reported along with the rest of the soldiers. I stood and looked at him, without saying a word.

"Listen, I'm sorry, but I don't deserve to be left behind," he pleaded.

"I don't trust you, and I'm not going out on any kind of mission with someone I don't trust," I said matter-of-factly. "Get inside." Yoni turned back and went inside, and we went out on patrol.

This patrol was better— the soldiers reacted well and didn't argue. We passed the town and reached a giant building which housed the regiment that covered the sector. The building was an old cigarette factory, and there were still plenty lying around. We were offered soft-pack Marlboro cigarettes, the kind you couldn't get in Israel at the time. Most of the guys didn't smoke. I took several packs, and felt like a looter.

Over the next few days, I transitioned into feral combat mode without any kind of conscious decision: I didn't shower, didn't take off my socks even when sleeping, ate little and only easily-digestible foods. I slept lightly, and stirred ready for action. I drank a ton of coffee. My senses were attuned and I was highly alert. I concentrated on the here-and-now, thinking in terms of missions and objectives. Exacting conduct, but very fulfilling: no ruminations, quick and sharp decision-making, everything very clear and incisive.

The following day, Yoni tried to report to the patrol again, and was promptly sent back to the kitchen. That evening, he came to talk to me. We spoke in a hall full of army cots, with combat gear strewn all over the place. He sat on the cot next to the one I had settled on, and moved the combat vest I had neatly placed around my helmet.

"How long is this punishment going to go on?" he asked.

"As far as I'm concerned, forever," I said with a coldness I didn't really feel.

"One little mistake and you're just gonna dump me on the side of the curb?"

"That wasn't a mistake, Yoni. Mistakes can be corrected, what you did cannot. You can disobey orders in the kitchen, not in the field."

I got up and walked away. Honestly, I kind of felt for him. I usually appreciate and admire defiance in people. But I couldn't let this one slide; not easily, at least. The soldiers, who were used to me being a laid-back and easygoing commander, were surprised. Some of them came up to me and tried to convince me to let him off the hook.

"I can't, guys," I said. "If I do, then each and every one of you will know in the back of your minds that you can refuse orders as well."

"You know that's not true. We always knew when to put jokes aside."

"True, but you don't this time," I said.

They were shocked that they couldn't convince me. Our relationship was usually such that I allowed myself to be convinced by logical reasoning.

During one of our night patrols, we felt pretty safe. We were walking down a narrow street, and the synchronized stomping sounds of our boots sounded like a coordinated march. That sound echoing through an Arab village at night stirred uncomfortable associations. Elad, who was at the back, suddenly yelled: "Eins! Zwei! Drei!" The team laughed in embarrassment. I didn't react. I instructed everyone to go into stealth mode, making the sounds of our boots inaudible. The weather was dreary, but it wasn't raining; just an occasional drizzle, not enough to saturate the sunbaked earth.

After three days in the kitchen, I went to see Yoni in the makeshift mess hall, filled with laminated folding tables and benches. Yoni was standing in the adjacent room, diligently scrubbing piles of huge pots. He was a physics student in his civilian life. I called him over. He sat in front of me, wiping his soapy hands dry.

"Yoni, do you understand why I couldn't overlook what you did?"

"I do," he answered laconically.

"Do you want to go back to operational duty?"

"What, and give all this up?" he looked around with an ironic smile.

"Yes, I'm sure that'll be hard, but duty calls."

"Do you want me to apologize to everyone?" he asked, slightly embarrassed.

"There's no need. We all get each other."

Yoni came back. The message was conveyed. I felt no need to humiliate him further.

One night, in the early hours of the morning, we set up a makeshift roadblock on the main road. The soldiers stopped two pedestrians walking down the road and inspected them. It was 4:30 AM, still pitch-black. Throughout the whole of the previous hour, only one car had passed by. It was cold, and we were in a sour mood.

"He's got a grenade in his pocket," the inspecting soldier suddenly said.

I quickly raised my weapon and said: "Shoot him." Luckily, he didn't. "Move. I'll shoot him," I said.

"Wait, it's just a warm yam. He must have kept it in his pocket," the inspector said.

The air flushed out of my lungs. I felt nauseous from the grave mistake I'd nearly made. I sat down and lit a cigarette. I was tired, cold, and worried. I was certain we had apprehended the person who had thrown a grenade at us during our first patrol. That was hardly enough to justify the fatal error Amir saved me from making.

At first light, we started climbing up towards the "kennels." That was the name we used for the sleeping quarters over the radio. We walked in night formation. Even though I thought about it, I was too tired to bother changing to open-field formation. The soldiers couldn't be bothered either. We walked back slumped and tired.

Suddenly we heard a faint noise of gunfire. "Enemy fire to our left!" someone yelled. Our immediate reaction was to turn left. Since we couldn't see who was shooting at us, we dropped to the ground. I realized we were too clustered, and not set up to engage in combat. I instructed the group to break into two squads, one to the left and one to the right. The soldiers reacted with expert skill, one rushing and two covering.

I've always felt like a lone warrior. The only way to successfully work as part of a team when you are a lone warrior is for everyone to know what you want, and for everyone to have the skills necessary to execute it. The team immediately demonstrated that that was the case. We rushed rapidly and skillfully, each covering for his other squad members. The source of fire was sparse, and our counter-fire destabilized the shooter.

We reached within thirty yards of the source of fire. I signaled for two soldiers to take out grenades. They glanced at each other to coordinate, and tossed their grenades simultaneously. "Grenade!" they yelled. Everyone lay down and counted— 21, 22, 23— two loud explosions came in rapid succession.

"Charge!" I yelled. I jumped to my feet and dashed forward. The soldiers fell into formation and charged forward, stopping every couple of steps to shoot at shoulder height before carrying on running. We reached the source. There was no body there, just some shells scattered on the ground, an empty AK-47 magazine, and a small pool of blood.

I looked around in search of runners. There was a house a couple of dozen yards down the hill. One of the soldiers yelled: "They must be in the house."

"Stop!" I said. "Count off basic numbers!" I yelled, to make sure no one was injured. The better option would have been to count off within the smaller squads, but I wanted to hear for myself. Everyone was okay. We changed magazines in gradual order[3], I left one squad behind to cover and led the other to the rear side of the house.

We stopped at the corner of a windowless wall. The soldiers formed a tight-knit line along the wall. I sent a full squad to the entrance. "Scan and enter, no grenade," I told them. We didn't know who was actually inside, it could have just been innocent civilians. The execution wasn't as seamless as it had been in the past, but satisfactory. They went and yelled: "Stairwell[4]."

I advanced and passed them. I sent a squad to scan the ground floor. It was empty. I called Yoni and we took the stairs, each covering the other's movement. We reached the second floor, which was split into two apartments. I sent Jacob with a squad to scan the apartment on the left while I and another squad entered the apartment to the right.

There was a family in the apartment. The children were crying, and the women were screaming. We moved

---

3   One soldier changes his magazine, and only when he's done does a second soldier change his, and so forth. That way, there is at least one soldier with a loaded magazine at all times.

4   The first soldier to look inside announces what he sees. There are different techniques to every layout, and the announcement informs which technique is to be employed. Every such announcement changes the course of action taken by the force.

along the walls. There were two openings in the room, one to our right and one in front of us. The family ran into the room to the right, but not to the one in front. I signaled the soldiers by slightly nodding my head towards the entrance. Yoni and Amir moved along both sides of the opening. I joined in behind Amir. I signaled— grenade. I didn't realize they had both taken out grenades and pulled out the safety pins until it was too late.

They both threw in the grenades with their elbows leaning on the doorpost— only then did I realize two grenades were being thrown instead of one. The first explosion came. Amir made a move to enter the room, but I grabbed his vest from behind and stopped him. Yoni leapt in, and the second grenade exploded. He was thrust out by the force of the explosion.

I stopped for a moment, then pushed Amir inside and followed him in. We sprayed the room with automatic fire, systematically covering every inch. "Magazine," I said, and knelt down. I changed magazines, and Amir followed suit. The dust started to settle, and we saw two armed boys, dead as doornails.

We rushed out to Yoni. He'd been hit by shrapnel in several places. We took off his shredded vest and looked for bleeding. The cover squad came in and the medic took over. We called for emergency evacuation.

We carried Yoni on a stretcher out to the yard outside the house. He was breathing heavily. I ordered the team into a circumferential defense formation. The helicopter asked for directions, and Jacob the signaler expertly instructed it. We could hear it getting closer. I looked at Yoni. His mouth was caked in blood. He smiled at me. I grabbed his hand, and it was cold as ice. Suddenly it started pouring rain. We lifted the stretcher to enter the building lobby, but just then, we heard the loud chopping sound of the helicopter rotor. We stood there as the pouring rain washed the blood off Yoni. After loading him to the chopper, we assembled in order and climbed back towards the "kennels," drained and exhausted.

I relieved the soldiers and laboriously made my way up to the second floor. I took off my gear, dropped it on the bed next to me, and sat down heavily on the sleeping bag that covered my bed. A strong hand grabbed my shoulder. Yossi sat next to me. We didn't say a word. He passed me a bottle of Zachlawi Arak he'd bought in the village. We drank straight from the bottle. When the bottle was half-empty, I crashed asleep.

The next morning, we learned that Yoni had died of his wounds on the way to the hospital. We all went to visit his family. None of us knew what to say. For months, I would wake up at night from nightmares in which I leave Yoni in the kitchen and he explodes there, or that I manage to stop him right before he enters a room full of monsters.

With time, the burden of guilt was dulled by the daily routine of study and work. Every year on the day of his death, we visit Yoni's grave and his family at their house. It always rains on that day.

CHAPTER 19

ENDGAME: SETTLING THE SCORE

Early 2000's. Erez sets out to get revenge.

Erez was concealed deep inside a thicket. He had been there for hours, waiting motionlessly, observing a building in the Arab settlement. He was less than 100 yards away; there was no need for binoculars. As evening came and darkness descended, he pulled out a pair of night-vision goggles from the bag behind his vest and put them up against his eyes. The image appeared in nuclear-green color. He disliked night-vision instruments, but this time he had no choice. The place was too dark, and the moon would only rise in a couple of hours.

Finally, he spotted some slight movement, followed by the sound of footsteps. Because of the distance, he had no way of knowing who the walking person was. Erez waited for him to approach the right house. In the meantime, he slowly made his way out of the thicket. Every time his uniform snagged on a thorn, he patiently removed it, until he was finally out.

Almost at the same time, the man reached the house. Erez snuck silently towards the house. When he reached the wall of the house, he stood motionlessly. He could hear hesitant voices inside. He took off the night-vision goggles and allowed his eyes to acclimate to the darkness. His pupils dilated, and he slowly made his way to the door, examining its axes and handle. He then stepped back, and then rushed at the door and burst it open. He found himself in a medium-sized room, which comprised the entire structure. Two men were sitting in front of him, brewing coffee on a small open fire. Erez lifted his rifle to his shoulder before the two could react to his intrusion.

"Turn to face me," he said in Arabic. One of them crouched down and picked something up off the ground. Erez recognized the shadow of an AK-47 assault rifle. He shot two rapid rounds at the man, and shifted his rifle in a small arch to face the second man, who was standing with his hands in the air.

Erez examined his face, and realized it didn't match up with any picture he knew. He instructed him to carefully go over to the corner, and walked over to the man lying in a pool of his own blood. He grabbed his leg and flipped him over. "Jack of Spades…" he mumbled.

Suddenly he heard hesitant voices approaching the door. He recognized the sound of a rifle hitting a helmet, and the sound of whispered orders. Without delay, he went to the corner of the structure, hung on a rafter beam and climbed up. The force burst in without shooting and scanned the room with flashlights. They found the wounded man and his terrified companion, continued to scan the room, and shouted orders in Hebrew. Having found nothing else, they removed the wounded man and his friend, and the ammunition they found lying around. Erez heard them scanning the perimeter, and slowly getting further and further away from the house.

He dropped back down to the floor. So you're following my chart, he thought to himself with slight amusement. He peered out, and when he saw the coast was clear, vanished into the darkness.

Eitan the brigade commander, the operations officer, the intelligence officer, and the deputy brigade commander sat in Eitan's office. The conversation was tense and heated.

"Maybe we should just let him go on. He's taking out our most-wanted list one by one," the operations officer said.

"First of all, that's very dangerous. He could get

himself killed, or worse— captured," the brigade commander said. "And secondly, he's not going to go over the list systematically. He's just making sure the system works before he applies it to his target."

"And what's his target?" the deputy brigade commander asked.

"Ibrahim Nasser. The Jack of Clubs."

"Why him?"

"He's the guy who sent the terrorist who killed Erez's children," Eitan said sternly.

"Did you know this before you reenlisted him?" the deputy brigade commander asked.

"I had a broad idea, but I didn't think it would become an obsession," Eitan said with slight hesitation.

"But you knew him from your regular service…" the deputy insisted.

"Yes, I did. He was my squad commander, he sent me to officer training. I guess I should have seen this coming," Eitan replied.

"So what do we do now?" asked the deputy brigade commander, who was the youngest man in the room.

"We help him," Eitan said with conviction.

"He doesn't seem to want any help," the deputy protested.

"He's going to want this help," Eitan said with a mysterious, smug smile.

***

Neta lay on the bed in the room adjacent to the office, passing the time waiting, certain he'd be back again. She was unsettled, angry, excited, and a bit scared by the flood of contradicting emotions washing over her. She felt she was playing a lead role in a Greek tragedy. The emotions made her young blood boil, stirred her maternal instincts, and irritated her senses.

After long, tense anticipation, she finally fell asleep. When she awoke, she felt someone watching her. She opened her eyes and saw a large, dark figure. She leapt out of bed and recognized it was Erez. He looked at her with sealed eyes, tired but curious.

She rushed over to hug him, remembering he had not objected last time. Erez recoiled slightly, but then returned her embrace. She felt his strong body and hands envelop her. She felt safe and secure, before noticing she was in fact very lightly dressed. She moved around in his arms, searching for his lips, and kissed him warmly.

He tightened his grip on her shoulders. She pulled back, and started undoing the buttons of his uniform shirt, revealing his muscular chest and stomach. Neta took off her top in one swift motion, and pressed her breasts up to his chest. She felt his pulse racing.

Erez swept her up and carried her to the narrow bed.

He took off her underwear and the rest of his clothes. She pressed up against him, kissing him with desperate passion. She felt their bodies merging, joining into one being. She screamed with pleasure as he moved on top of her, and erupted into an orgasm like she had never felt before. Later, she lay on top of him, both of them naked and sleepy.

"You remind me of someone," he whispered half-asleep.

"We have the same eyes and breasts," she said.

Erez opened his eyes in surprise, trying to fathom what she had just said. He sat up and looked at her incredulously.

"I'm Liat's daughter. Didn't you notice my last name?" she asked.

Erez looked slightly frightened, calculating something in his mind.

"Don't worry, silly. I'm not your daughter. The numbers don't add up." He sat up as well, hugged and kissed her.

Erez broke away, put on his pants, and went into the adjacent office. When Neta came in herself, she saw him sitting in front of the map and tables making calculations on a piece of paper.

"Did you update the data?" he asked.

"Of course," she answered, offended by the sharp change of tone. "Do you want to eat?" she asked. "I brought some food from lunch."

Erez wolfed down his food in silence while jotting down numbers and symbols on a piece of paper. Finally he leaned back, pulled out a cigarette and lit it. Neta sat in front of him, silent.

"Don't take this personally. I don't really understand what I'm feeling right now," he said.

"I know exactly what I feel, though," she said, clearly offended.

"I'm sorry, all of this just suddenly crashed into my life. I thought I was settling scores, now suddenly I'm opening new ones."

"I'm not a score."

"No, you certainly aren't. You're something wonderful that I'm not sure I deserve right now..." he said.

Neta got up and hugged him, and Erez hugged her back. He then got up, packed some things, kissed her, and disappeared.

***

Eitan scrutinized the eleven middle-aged, sloppily-uniformed soldiers in front of him. Some of them looked in excellent shape, especially those who had continued to serve in the security forces. The others were reasonably fit for their age. Eitan knew there was no substitute for experience and familiarity. They arrived in response to the emergency warrant he had sent them and an urgent phone call from him.

"So what is it, Shoelace?" Jacob asked, referring to Eitan by his old nickname.

Eitan felt everybody's eyes on him. He was the only one in full uniform, including his colonel rank insignias. He knew all of them, but they had lost contact years ago. The group had carried on together, performing operations and going on reserve duty, while he took a different path and climbed up the command hierarchy.

"I called you in on an emergency warrant because Erez disappeared a couple of days ago. Since his disappearance, three wanted terrorists with blood on their hands have been killed. Nobody knows who killed them," Eitan said.

The guys looked around at each other. Some cracked a smile.

"So Erez has gone vigilante," Assi said. "Son of bitch, he's the man."

"He's doing what we'd all love to do," Amir mumbled in satisfaction.

"It's about time."

"Okay, so what do you need us to do?" Jacob asked.

"You can probably assume we're not going to help you catch him," Amir said.

"No, guys, I want to help him," Eitan said. "I want

you to find him and join him. I believe he's out to get the man who killed his children, and I don't want him going after him alone."

"Okay, but how do we find him? I mean, this is the man who taught all of us how to hide."

"I'd check in with the officer who worked with him," Eitan said with a smile.

"No kidding. That fast?"

"Well, he was always good."

"I'm not one hundred percent certain, but I think there's something going on there. Do you guys remember Liat?" Eitan said.

"That older chick who turned his head? What about her?"

"That's her daughter."

"And you knew this?"

"Of course not, I just recently figured it out. I'm not sure Erez knows," Eitan concluded.

***

The reserve team entered Neta's office. She looked up in surprise, seeing a bunch of middle-aged reserve soldiers with weapons and vests they had just signed for. They settled into the empty rooms, organizing their equipment— fitting instruments to their vests, scopes to their rifles, and sharpening knife blades with whetting stones. Some of them were brewing coffee on a portable burner in the middle of the room.

"Would you mind telling me who you are and what you're doing here?" Neta asked.

"We're Erez's team. Do you know where we could find him? Or, can you convey a message to him?"

Neta stood in silence, slightly embarrassed.

"I-I think he'll come back tonight," she said.

The guys exchanged joyful looks. "What makes you say that?"

"Just a hunch," she said.

"Did he come here before?"

"Yeah, a couple of times."

"Well, that is his weakness."

"What is?"

"Loyalty."

As evening descended, the team passed the time reading maps and speculating on Erez's whereabouts. Yigal stood in front of the tables and charts, examining them for a long time. He called Ami over. They two of them went over the numbers and equations. Yigal sat and started jotting down calculations.

"What're you doing, Yigal?"

"Testing it."

"But you don't know arithmetic."

"That's right. But this is not arithmetic, this is proper math. And it's not bad at all."

"Yigal has a Ph.D. in mathematics. He shouldn't even be here…" someone explained to Neta.

At dinnertime, they headed out to the mess hall. Neta went to roam around outside. Suddenly he appeared next to her. As soon as she recognized him, she hugged him and he hugged her back.

"What's going on in there?" he whispered.

"Your team is here, and they're preparing to help you."

Erez didn't say anything, and gave her a long kiss. She melted in his arms, feeling his longing and desire. When the team got back, they came into the office. After some pats on the back and shaking of hands, Erez and the team sat down to look at the maps.

"So how do you want to do this?" Jacob asked, ready for action.

"Tomorrow morning he's due to pick up an explosives belt from a sewing workshop that makes them. He's probably not going to come alone. The volunteer who's supposed to blow himself up will accompany him."

"How do we know this?"

"Information and statistical calculations."

"Okay, well, about that— you have a slight miscalculation. It comes out much lower than you thought, something in the vicinity of seventy percent," Yigal said solemnly.

"I'm definitely not gonna argue math with you, but I think that refers more to the particular hour than to the likelihood of the meeting taking place in general," Erez answered.

"Yes, the chances vary throughout the day. The best chances are in the early morning. By the way, kudos on the idea. It's brilliant, converting information into statistics," Yigal lauded his old commander.

"That was part of my start-up venture," Erez muttered with his gaze firmly fixed on the floor.

"Maybe it could be revived. You have an experiment here that seems to be working."

"That's not what I'm here for," Erez said.

"So what are you here for, really?"

"I'm here to kill the son of a bitch who murdered my children," Erez said with fire in his eyes.

"Maybe we'll find his family and kill them, in return."

"We don't fight kids," Erez said.

They went over the plan. Erez sketched the four-story building located in the center of town. The workshop was on the fourth floor, hard to reach.

"We'll need to leave soon. I'm going to Eitan to get the stuff we need," Jacob said.

"Roll call in two hours."

***

The team gathered in Erez's office at midnight. Eitan appeared without his insignias, equipped with a vest and weapon. The team felt uncomfortable with his presence.

"I'm only here to coordinate," he said. "I've prepared a motorized evacuation. I'll be with it."

He assigned their radio networks, shook their hands, and left.

"Guys," Erez said in a low voice, "none of you have to be here. This is my revenge," he made it clear.

"It's ours too. Go on with the inspection."

"I trust you have your equipment in check."

"Are you slacking off? Check."

After inspecting the gear, they got on a truck and drove off. Just before they left, Erez went to Neta and gave her a long hug.

"Come back in one piece," she pleaded.

"That's not possible. I'm already broken," he replied.

"For me…" she said, and kissed him.

He turned around and left, leaving her standing there with tears in her eyes.

***

The team approached the town and stopped at its

outskirts. They fell into formation, and snuck into the town along the axis they had prepared.

After about half an hour, they reached the vicinity of the building. Sharon fasted himself to a rope, and started scaling the outside of the building. When he reached the roof, he pulled up the rope and anchored it to the floor. One by one, the team climbed up, some of them just barely making it. An hour later, they were all crouched on the roof. They situated themselves so that they could not be seen from below. The building was the tallest in the area, so they couldn't be spotted from other rooftops either. They lay down and waited.

At 5:30 AM, the floor below them started coming to life. At 6 AM, they fixed the explosive device to the roof, and detonated it at 6:15 AM. A thunderous explosion tore through the morning mist, and a huge hole gaped in the building's roof. They suspended themselves from the edge of the roof, and jumped in. Two team members sprained their ankles and remained behind to cover. They scanned the rooms quickly. They encountered an armed terrorist in the second room and shot him down quickly. In the back room, they found three suspects hiding. They cuffed their hands, as they did everyone else in the building.

"Erez, your client is in the back room!" Jacob said, pointing his thumb at a steel door.

Erez walked into the room, accompanied by two team members. The men sat cuffed in plastic zip-ties. Erez examined the three.

"Get them out of here," he pointed at two of them.

He went to the corner of the room, took off his vest, and laid it on the ground. He placed his weapon on top of it. He immediately recognized that Ibrahim Nasser, the man responsible for murdering his children, the man he had been hunting down, was the man left sitting in the room. He pulled out his knife and approached him. Ibrahim desperately tried to crawl back. Erez reached him, grabbed his hands, and cut off the zip-tie.

"Stand up!" he shouted in Arabic. "Do you know who I am?"

"A Jew dog!" Ibrahim brazenly replied.

"Yes. A dog that's about to kill you."

Erez threw his knife towards his vest, and squared up to Ibrahim. He punched him in the face using his left fist. Ibrahim pounced on him in a fit of fury. Erez forced him back with a series of rapid left jabs. Ibrahim continued advancing, wildly striking at Erez's hand and shoulder. Erez grabbed Ibrahim's chin with his left hand, and landed a tremendous sickle blow—starting from his leg, advancing to his hip and shoulder, and culminating with an iron fist. "The Erez Sledgehammer," his opponents used to call the move. His fist exploded into Ibrahim's ribs. Erez let him go and delivered two rapid blows, one from the left and one from the right, and finished with an uppercut which channeled all the rage burning inside him. The blow hit Ibrahim square on the chin, and he collapsed to the ground.

Erez towered over him, panting heavily from the sudden burst of exertion, and the adrenaline furiously pumping through his veins. He then turned to the door. Ibrahim seized the opportunity to pounce again, sinking his teeth deep into Erez's calf. Erez could feel the teeth tearing his muscle, and the blood running down his leg. He turned around and struck Ibrahim's blood-soaked head repeatedly until he finally let go. After releasing himself, Erez slumped down. Ibrahim leaped to his feet again, and with his face smeared in blood, sent a kick towards Erez's head. Erez noticed the leg moving towards his head from the corner of his eye, grabbed Ibrahim's foot and sharply twisted it, turning a screw on three joints at once: the hip, the knee, and the ankle. Ibrahim fell on his face. Without hesitation, ignoring the pain in his calf, Erez held onto the rotated foot, got up, and leapt forward towards Ibrahim's back. He landed on the back of his knee. The immense pressure shattered Ibrahim's knee. His mutilated leg became as shapeless and empty as a sack of rags.

Erez turned him over, sat on top of him, and began

pulverizing his face with punches, left and right, again and again, in a fit of uncontrollable fury which erupted from deep inside him. Ibrahim tried to block the blows with his hand. Erez grabbed his wrist and broke it with one violent twist.

Ibrahim's face was reduced to a pulpy mash of blood. "Blood! Blood!" an incredible force roared inside Erez's mind. His fists were stained with blood. The image of his children's faces flashed before his eyes, covered in blood. Erez stopped punching, grabbed Ibrahim's neck, and started squeezing the life out of him. He thought about his children blown up on that bus. He was haunted by the image. But then he heard Neta's desperate whisper: "Come back in one piece..."

Erez let go of Ibrahim and labored up to his feet. He went to the corner, put on his vest and weapon, and put the knife back in its sheath. He walked back over to Ibrahim, grabbed his other foot, and dragged him out of the room.

There was a commotion outside. Eitan arrived with the backup force and raided the building. He saw Erez dragging Ibrahim.

"Is that him?" Eitan asked.

"Yes, that's him," Erez confirmed.

"Is he dead?"

"No. Take him to prison," Erez said. He let go of

Ibrahim's leg and walked towards the stairs.

He got out of the building, and sat down in the car. A medic attended to his torn calf muscle. A couple of minutes later, his team joined up with him, two with sprained ankles and one with a cut on his cheek. They drove away through a raging mob. A few minutes later, the building that was used to make explosive belts exploded. When they reached the camp, Erez asked Eitan: "Where's the bastard?"

"What bastard?" Eitan played dumb.

"Not funny, Eitan," Erez said sternly. "Ibrahim Nasser, the son of a bitch I made the mistake of leaving only half-dead."

"Oh. I accidently forgot him inside the exploded building…" Eitan answered with a straight face.

Erez looked at him without saying a word.

"That's what friends are for," Eitan said. He patted Erez on the back, and went back to command the brigade. Erez sat down on a rock, looked around, and saw his team heading to return their equipment. Neta stood at the door and looked at him. Soon, he'd get up and go to the office. But for now, he just wanted to understand whether he'd settled the score, or just opened it.

CHAPTER 20

EPILOGUE: EREZ AND ME

We sat on a desolate beach in the north of the Dead Sea, a couple of six-packs of Heineken casually placed beside us. We had drunk about half already, and smoked cigarettes. Neta ran towards us on the beach. She really was a sight to behold, especially in her swimsuit.

"You're a lucky guy," I told him.

"At the end of the day, I'm lucky. But it always balances out."

"I always hated the end of Book of Job. As if the new wife and kids somehow made up for the ones he lost."

"Justice is not part of the deal. If you want justice, you have to take it yourself."

"You know you don't really exist, right?" I said, slightly envious.

"The way I see it, I'm more real than you are."

"You're a fictional character in a book," I insist.

"And you're a grumpy old man."

"I think I'll stuff you back into the box I took you out of."

"You can't. It's out of your hands now."

"You believe that?"

"You will too, soon enough."

"Take another beer. Get pissed."

"By the way, I'm thinking about adding a bit where the army buys your patent for the search algorithm."

"Don't bother, that's not credible. The army doesn't work that logically."

"Okay. So I'll send you back to catch a few more terrorists."

Neta reached us, her skin glimmering with sweat. She was panting, her impressive breasts bobbing up and down.

"Eitan says you have twelve more terrorists waiting for you," she said.

"I told you."

"Of course you told me. You're writing this."

Done, but not finished.

Made in United States
Troutdale, OR
11/24/2023

14881906R00156